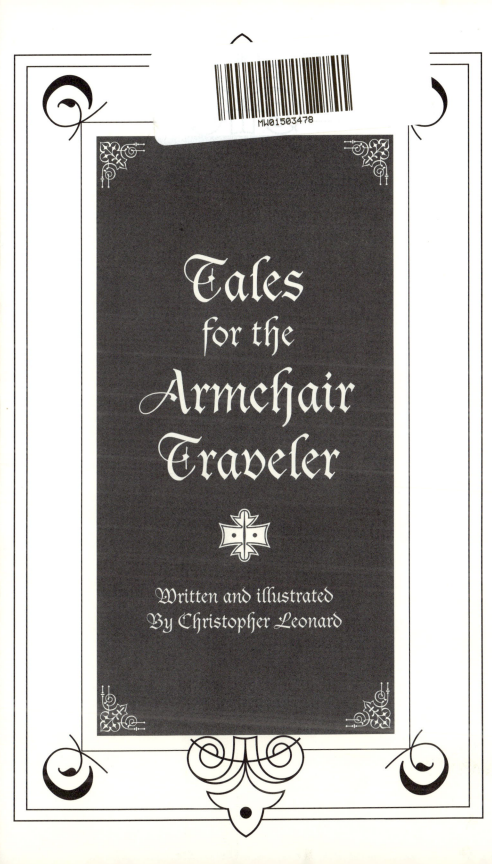

Tales
for the
Armchair
Traveler

Written and illustrated
By Christopher Leonard

Published in the United States by Richmond Hill Inn

First Printing, December 2002

Copyright: December 2002 by Richmond Hill Inn
All Rights Reserved

ISBN 0-9725857-0-2

Book designed by Ginger Graziano
Edited by Melissa Stanz

Printed in the United States of America

To Dr. Albert J. Michel,

World adventurer

CONTENTS

ACKNOWLEDGEMENTS

These stories are about journeys, and happily, I did not take this journey alone. Many thanks to Mark File, Director of Marketing at Richmond Hill Inn, for his tireless efforts on behalf of this publication. Thanks also to Margaret Michel for her expert advice on illustrations. Finally, I must express gratitude for the quick eye of my editor Melissa R. Stanz, and the creativity and taste of Ginger Graziano, the book designer.

FOREWARD

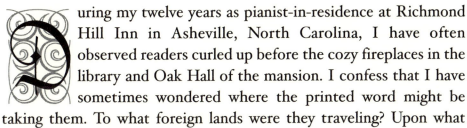uring my twelve years as pianist-in-residence at Richmond Hill Inn in Asheville, North Carolina, I have often observed readers curled up before the cozy fireplaces in the library and Oak Hall of the mansion. I confess that I have sometimes wondered where the printed word might be taking them. To what foreign lands were they traveling? Upon what marvelous adventures had they embarked?

These stories were written with those readers in mind. They are most certainly NOT children's stories, though they are mostly childlike. Their sole intention is to amuse adults. So, without further ado, I bid you, "Bon Voyage!"

Chapter 1

TIBOO AND CREATION

N THE BEGINNING, ACCORDING TO THE ABORIGINES, THERE was "Dreamtime." Then it was that all of Creation was sung into being. People arrived on the scene and begat more people. They existed in harmony with the earth, so that the world was still joyfully singing generations later, when two brothers lived in what is today known as the Northern Territory of Australia.

Oodna, the older brother, was the strongest and tallest member of his tribe. He excelled at the hunt and in battle, and he helped provide his community with food and protection. In turn, the people valued him, and he brought much honor to his parents.

His parents were also proud of their younger son Tiboo, though for different reasons. Shorter and more sensitive than his brother, Tiboo had little success wielding a spear or boomerang, and he could not stomach the violence of war. He made up for these deficiencies, however, by means of his artistic skills. He wove baskets, sang, and mimicked the kookaburra. He played the didgeridoo and added a few dance steps to the ritual repertoire. He was best known for his cave paintings, and everyone agreed that his spirals were the most hypnotic they'd ever seen.

Oodna eventually took a wife and began a family. He did not approve of Tiboo's urge to communicate in grandiose ways, for he, himself, believed that silence befitted a warrior and speech defiled a sacred hunt. When he saw that his parents were charmed by Tiboo's show-off antics, Oodna grew disgusted and took his wife and children to live on the edge of the tribal territory.

3

Tiboo returned his brother's rejection, and a chill settled over the complex kinships that made up the community. One day, Tiboo could stand the tension no longer. He bid farewell to his parents and headed west into the outback. Everyone told him he would die, that he would suffer the consequences of his rash action, but a spirit was calling him to solitude.

It is true that no one was less suited for the wilderness than Tiboo. A naïve, flighty fellow, he was happy prey for sun, foe, and beast. He would have perished within days, had he not the guidance of his spirits and the help of the animals and trees.

After a few hours of wandering, Tiboo grew hungry and stopped in the shade of a eucalyptus to ponder his plans for lunch. It so happened that this eucalyptus was partial to gossip, and high in its branches lived a koala that was given to conversation. Together, they chatted away their days and were always delighted to speak to strangers.

"G'day, Tiboo!" the eucalyptus said.

"How do you know my name?" asked Tiboo.

"Aw, 'e knows everything," the koala answered, and then he sighed. "It's the wind what tells 'im all the latest news."

"The wind isn't my only source," said the eucalyptus. "I'm a magnet for gossip; a shoulder for the world to cry on. Go ahead ask me something, anything at all. I promise I'll know the answer. Wouldn't you love to know the dirt on somebody? Go on! Ask me something!"

"Very well, I'll ask you something," Tiboo agreed. "Where can I find some food around these parts?"

"What sort of question is that?" The eucalyptus sniffed haughtily, and folded its two lowest branches close to its trunk. "Pfft!"

"I'd say it's a fine question," Tiboo said, smiling, "if one happens to be famished."

"It's MUNDANE!" insisted the eucalyptus, and he shuddered

with revulsion. "I'll never understand the obsession some creatures have for food. I need only minerals, water, and warmth. This koala, on the other hand, never stops stripping my beautiful, fragrant leaves to shove them down his greedy mouth. I can see you're a similar type, Tiboo. I suppose the pair of you will have me bald by the end of the afternoon."

"I don't want your leaves," Tiboo assured him.

"Why not, mate?" asked the koala. "They're awfully good leaves."

"They certainly are!" shouted the eucalyptus, his pride wounded. "They're the best leaves on the whole continent."

"I'm sure they are," Tiboo said, "but I had something more substantial in mind."

"You don't want to eat ME, do you?" the koala asked, gripping the bark and quivering from head to claw. "Oh, dear."

"No," Tiboo told him, "I don't believe in taking the life of any sort of creature."

"Oh, that's all right then, mate," said the koala, slowly wiping his brow. "I say, what if I toss you down a few of these tree-worms, eh? They're silly creatures, and don't even know they's alive."

"Uh, I dunno..."

"Aw, come on!" the koala said, and he began flinging worms to the ground. "It's the worms what'll eat you, in the end, so take your revenge today, mate!"

Tiboo gorged himself on the worms and felt satisfied. He thanked the eucalyptus and koala for their hospitality and conversation. To show his gratitude, he painted a spiral on the trunk of the eucalyptus. Then he waved good-bye and resumed his journey.

As the afternoon wore on, and the sun continued to beat down on the red earth, Tiboo grew listless. He decided to nap beneath a bottle tree to restore his energy and clarity of mind. He had just drifted off to sleep when a kangaroo stopped by and began punching him in the face, ears, and belly.

"Hey, what's the big idea?" cried Tiboo, in horror.

"Put 'em up, up, up!" challenged the kangaroo, as he sparred at the air. "Put 'em up, up, up!"

Tiboo tried to crawl away, but the kangaroo dragged him back and jumped on his solar plexus. The commotion disturbed the bottle tree, who was sleeping off a hangover. The bottle tree groaned and reached forth a limb to block a ray of sunshine.

"Thay, wath all thith noith?" the bottle tree demanded, his sap still flowing with alcohol. "Can't a tree get a little theep around here?"

"We're having a bit of sport, is all," the kangaroo said, jerking Tiboo to his feet and punching him hard in the arm. "No hard feelings, right mate?"

"None at all." Tiboo clutched his stomach and bent double with pain. "Just a bit of sport."

"There, you see!" the kangaroo said to the bottle tree. "So you can just pipe down and pass out again."

"But I can't theep with you guyth rough-houthing," whined the bottle tree, punctuating his complaint with a hiccup and belch. "You'll have to find thomewhere elth to play."

"Look, I'm in need of a wink, meself," Tiboo said, "and I don't see any other shade in the vicinity."

"Never fear!" the kangaroo said, flexing his biceps. "I can save the day! Jump in my pouch, and I'll take you, express, to the next tree."

Tiboo consented. He thanked the bottle tree for what little hospitality it had shone, and then, to show his largesse, he painted a handsome spiral on the tree's trunk. He then climbed into the kangaroo's pouch, and they took off at breakneck speed across the rugged terrain. In what seemed like no time at all, Tiboo was deposited beneath a welcoming grove of shade trees.

A few weeks later, Tiboo reached what was known as "the perishing land," a vast desert with little vegetation and temperatures that soared to punishing extremes. Soon, Tiboo was desperate for water and shade, but he could see nothing about him except parched land, nests of snakes, and low, brittle brush. Just as he was losing hope, a lone dingo came to his aid.

"You know," the dingo said, as he casually scratched his butt against a rock, "if I was a speculating fellow, I'd say you were about done for."

"Don't trouble yourself about it, friend," Tiboo rasped. "When I am gone, you must make a meal of me."

"You?" The dingo hooted with laughter and rolled about in the red dust. "You wouldn't even make a decent snack! Hee-hee-hee-hee! There's not a morsel 'a meat on ya, mate! Not even enough to roast on a stick. Hee-hee-hee-hee!"

"You needn't be so merry about it," deadpanned Tiboo. "Oh, well, do as you please. I'd rather go hearing laughter than sobs. I think I'll paint my last spiral on this rock, then curl beneath this bush to die."

"I'll keep you company," the dingo said, plopping down beside him.

Tiboo completed his painting and immediately proclaimed it the best of his work. The dingo conceded that it was unique, but he seemed puzzled by it too. He paced before it, turning his head to one side and then the other.

"What's it supposed to be?" he asked Tiboo.

"Nothing...and everything."

"Is it magical?"

"Oh, I think it probably is."

"Well, it's unique, anyway," the dingo said, as he lifted his leg on a pitiful piece of scrub. "I suppose I shouldn't leave a gifted artist to die in the wilderness. Tell ya what, hop on my back, and I'll take you to a lovely stream that's just over that ridge there."

"I'm afraid I'd be too large a passenger, but thank you for offering."

"Nonsense!" protested the dingo. "I've carried fleas that

weighed more than you. Hee-hee-hee-hee!"

Tiboo sat on the dingo's back, and they dashed and darted across the hot desert. As the full moon rose over their heads, they reached a gushing stream in a deep ravine. Tiboo refreshed himself, and the dingo took off with Tiboo's heartfelt thanks and a sack of painted rocks.

It was in this way, with the help of his spirits and all of Creation, that Tiboo was rescued again and again from discomfort and the jaws of death. He wandered many years, knowing more happiness than despair. He eventually succumbed to the elements, as his tribespeople had predicted; but he lived more years than anyone had supposed, including himself.

Time marched on, and the ancient song continued. Then the Europeans came, and most folks ceased to listen to Creation. Oodna's descendants were forced to trek further and further west. As they traveled, they pointed to the painted rocks and said, "Look! Crazy 'ol Tiboo was here!"

Chapter 2

NICOLAUS AND APHRODITE

THENS WAS BESIEGED AND LIKELY TO CAPITULATE AT ANY hour. Her cultivated countryside had been trampled and burned; her once-mighty navy had been destroyed at the battle of Aegospotami; and her innovative democracy had been strangled by war, plague, and demagoguery. The Third Peloponnesian War was coughing to a close.

In the Spartan camp, there were few signs of impending victory: no toasts, no cheers, no bawdy songs; not even a relaxation of discipline. These men had been trained for war and only war since age seven. Their lives belonged to the state, and they obeyed without question. They were—to a man—confident they had conquered the tyranny of their emotions. Even so, anticipation quietly vibrated through them. After twenty-seven years of war, the hour neared when they would glean the harvest of their labor. They would plunder the streets of Athens, their ancient rival, and strip her of arrogance and treasure.

One of these warriors—a cavalry officer named Nicolaus—was chagrinned to find himself ripped away from the table before the meal was served. In the last days of the siege, with the promise of loot palatable, Nicolaus was reassigned to a vast estate in eastern Attica. The time for destruction had passed, he was told, and the time for restoration was dawning. If the Spartan occupation of Athens was going to succeed, it would need sustenance from the countryside. Nicolaus' mission was to repair the war-torn vineyards on the estate and convince the aristocrats who owned the place that Spartan law was superior to democracy.

To help him get the job done, Nicolaus was allotted a dozen

warriors, ten helots, fifteen Athenian captives, and three advisors trained, respectively, in engineering, architecture, and agricultural planning. He also took along his personal slave, and his adjutant, Telemus, a fine horseman and something of a friend since their days together in the Gymnopaedia.

The journey was not long, but longer than necessary. The captives not only hindered speed with their reluctant paces but also spurred the helots to disgruntlement. Nicolaus and his men managed to quash physical rebellion, but the murmuring and resentment continued.

The estate was in shambles. The vines had been cut, burned, and, in places, uprooted. A wing of the villa had collapsed, and its marble walls stained with soot and graffiti. The gardens had been trodden by the feet of a thousand warriors, and a statue of Bacchus had been decapitated and toppled from its terrace pedestal.

A slave boy, who seemed deficient in sense, was thrown out of the villa to greet the arriving party. He scrambled into the courtyard and fell onto the earth, in obeisance. He recited a message from his master, Polyeuctus, who welcomed the Spartans in the name of Zeus. Were they, the slave boy nervously inquired, planning to stay long?

Nicolaus dismounted and kicked the boy out of his way. He drew his sword, called for Telemus to join him, and stormed into the villa. Inside, he found a temple to decadence, littered with marble, art, and detail—all of it void of function. Nicolaus despised Athenian knick-knacks, and disgust swelled within him. He found his way into the atrium and shouted for Polyeuctus. Again and again he shouted, until two slaves, fearful for their lives, dragged their master from his hiding and threw him at the feet of the Spartans.

"Spare me!" cried Polyeuctus. "I am nearly fifty!"

He looked it and more. He was wrinkled and overweight, and his hair needed dressing. To the Spartans, nothing was a surer sign of debauchery than unkempt hair. They dressed their own, incessantly.

"Silence, you swine!" Nicolaus snarled, as he removed his fearsome-looking bronze helmet. "Do you want to live to see fifty-one?"

Other members of the household were rounded up and brought into the atrium. These included: Polyeuctus' wife, Hippodamia, who was even broader than her husband; a daughter, Ocyrrhoe, who seemed to match the combined weight of her parents; and an old, blind, and senile granny. There were, in addition, seven slaves, who were slovenly, tubby, and stinky.

"By the gods!" swore Nicolaus. "How did you keep so fat in war time?"

"Fat?" Hippodamia glared at him. "I'll have you know I've lost sixty-nine pounds since the wars began."

"How revolting," Nicolaus managed to comment, though his washboard abdominals heaved. "Why aren't you behind the city walls? Don't you follow the laws of your own state?"

"We took refuge in Athens for many months, sir," Polyeuctus explained, "but we fled after plague broke out. We had to, sir, for the sake of our daughters."

"Oh, you've no idea what it was like, young man!" Hippodamia threw up her hands and spread herself upon a couch, as though at a party. "There was never enough to eat in the city. Never, never, never! And if one managed to snatch a scrap or two, one ate it, at once, or fought off the rats. And the stench from the corpses piled high in the streets! Oh, it was dreadful, young man, and you would have fled as quickly!"

"Daughters," repeated Nicolaus. "Polyeuctus, you did say 'daughters', didn't you? Have you another daughter besides Ocyrrhoe?"

"We had eight children before these cursed wars," Polyeuctus told him. "Six of them sons. A father never hoped for better sons. All of them gone now."

"Three died at Potidaea," said Hippodamia, wiping her tears away with her fists. "Two more were drowned off the coast of Syracuse, and the youngest..." She broke off, unable to continue.

"The youngest was cut down by the plague," Polyeuctus whispered, patting his wife's hand. "He was a golden tyke, that one. Our favorite, wasn't he, Hippodamia? Yes, we hated to lose him. Only six years old. We couldn't hold and comfort him because of his contagion. We put him out the door and left him to die in the street."

"And the other daughter?" asked Nicolaus. "Is she dead?"

"Oh, no, sir!" A smile replaced Polyeuctus' contorted grieving. "Phobe is very much alive! She's likely playing down by the sacred stream, isn't she, Ocyrrhoe? That's where Phobe goes to be alone. She's a strange young woman, really, but so lively!"

"Telemus, go and find the other daughter," Nicolaus told his adjutant. "And you, slaves, get to the kitchens and prepare some food! My men are hungry."

Polyeuctus was a weasly fellow, no doubt about it, but resourceful. To keep food on his family's table, he bribed the cook at the nearest Spartan outpost, and thereby maintained a supply of grain and oil for his larder. He trapped all manner of birds and kept them in an aviary, from which he personally selected a victim for his plate each day. He sent his slaves down to the sea to fish for every sort of aquatic creature, and they always returned because, after all, where else were they to find such a table laid in wartime? And if the family's palate had been stretched to the point of bizarre, due to previous deprivation, then at least, the sauces were dependable. The meal set before the Spartans was nothing short of a feast.

Wine was in abundance at the table, and Nicolaus deduced that the vineyards were not completely destroyed. That meant less work for him. He'd already begun organizing things in his mind. He planned to drive the slaves during the day and lecture the family on Spartan ideals at night. Self-restraint evidently eluded them, whatever their hardships.

While the aristocrats lounged on their couches, sucked grease from their fingers, and drank deeply from their wine bowls, Nicolaus began to orate. He had only touched on the subject of Lycurgus when he was interrupted by an amazing series of events.

Telemus returned with the youngest daughter Phobe, and she was wonderfully unlike her family. She glowed with health and pulsed with youth. Her body was trim and firm, suggesting athletic prowess, and her economy of motion and fearless eye contact told Nicolaus that this was a no nonsense woman, unmarred by Athenian affectations.

Who knows how the cavalry officer would have responded to Phobe, had he been left to his own free will? He might have loved her, or he might have dismissed her. His heart could have melted or hardened. Perhaps he had no freewill; perhaps he knew only the will of the state. If this was so, he needed divine help to change him, and divine help is what he got—in the form of Aphrodite.

The goddess appeared amidst the fluttering of doves and a swirling shower of rose petals. Her figure was voluptuous, and she seemed proud of every pound. She kept stroking her naked flesh, which was as pale as the moon and sparkling with gold dust. Her eyes, the color of the Aegean, sought out Nicolaus and froze him on the spot. Having rendered him helpless, she took cruel pleasure in ridiculing him.

"Look at our Spartan hero now," she taunted, squeezing his lips into a purse with her fingers. "What do you suppose is going on in that handsome head of his, hm? Is he thinking of virginal maidens, enticing harridans, or even me—the goddess of love? No, I tell you. He's thinking of war. Always war!"

"Oh, magnificent goddess," begged Polyeuctus, on his knees, "you know we have honored you in this house. Please defend us! Send this Spartan back to Athens, for he's a mad fanatic who will not rest until he has put an end to leisure and beauty!"

"I have a better idea," Aphrodite said, so sweetly that the hair stood on the back of Polyeuctus' neck. "I cannot return him to Athens to kill, maim, and pillage. Love, alone, will stem his violence, and only love will mock his pride. I shall turn this machine into a lover."

"Never!" shouted Telemus, drawing his sword. "All of Sparta knows of your villany, Aphrodite! Your schemes to rob heroes of their glory! I won't let you emasculate the noble Nicolaus!"

15

"Hah, you cannot stop me!" Aphrodite froze Telemus with her eyes, just as he raised his sword against her. "There. That's how a man should be—pretty and silent."

The other Spartans screamed and fled, leaving Aphrodite to her whims. She circled the two paralyzed warriors, drumming her fingernails against their breastplates and complimenting them on the fine shape of their legs. Then she grew bored with the company of mortals, and drawing herself into a high-dramatic attitude, she issued her commands.

"Nicholaus shall fall in love with Phobe, and she with him," the goddess proclaimed, deaf to the protests of Polyeuctus and his family. "As for the presumptuous Telemus, he shall love Ocyrrhoe. Let it be as I say!"

With this she vanished, along with her doves and rose petals. Nicolaus and Telemus were restored to animation. And what animation! Telemus fell at Ocyrrhoe's big feet, and he wept with joy at the sight of her "beauty." He kissed her toes and fingertips and strained to sweep her into his arms. He faltered under the weight of her, and they both fell hard to the floor. They exploded into laughter and took to lusty wrestling.

Nicolaus and Phobe were similarly smitten, but their natures were cool and courtly. They were hesitant to touch, lest passion overcome them. For a while, they stood lost in each other's eyes, until Nicolaus took Phobe's hands in his and softly, ever so softly, swore his eternal devotion.

Polyeuctus was bewildered. On the one hand, his daughters were about to be defiled by Spartans, but on the other hand, the family was gaining the protection of the conquerors. There would be no more fires in the vineyards. There would be plenty of food. Perhaps all would be well.

Everything was well...for a time. The lovers were wed, and Polyeuctus and Hippodamia soon had grandchildren. The vineyards returned to life, and the villa was repaired and expanded. The Spartans began to laugh more often, drink more wine, and sing ballads rather than war songs. Their discipline grew lax, and their waists grew thicker.

They started treating the slaves with some measure of compassion, and they freed their Athenian captives. Love had transformed them.

But alas, mortals in those days were at the mercy of the gods. One misty winter day, nearly two years after Athens had fallen, Ares paid a visit to the estate. Not wishing to be recognized as the god of war, he came dressed as a fortune–teller. The happy family welcomed him into their home.

At the table that evening, Ares outwardly smiled, but inwardly cringed. He considered mortals to be no more than pawns in the great game of the gods— a game that his former lover Aphrodite was winning. His glorious Peloponnesian Wars were over, and he had another twenty years to go before the birth of Phillip of Macedon. This hiatus from death and destruction depressed Ares. He felt deprived and impotent.

Although he couldn't indulge in war, he could dabble in mischief. He set his mind on causing grief to Polyeuctus' family and came with that purpose. The longer he sat dining with them, the more nauseated he became. Their kindness, cheerfulness, and above all, their disgusting affection were more than he could stand. He shocked them by pounding his fists on the table and calling for his current lover Enyo.

With a puff of sulfur, Enyo, the goddess of war, appeared. She was pretty, but something of a tart. Her hair hung down to her kneecaps; her breasts were melon-size; and her cosmetics tastelessly applied. Her taste in friends was equally dubious, for with her came Terror, Trembling, and Panic. They opened their mouths, and the din of a thousand souls in agony poured into the room. Enyo snapped her fingers, and the screaming abruptly ceased.

"Ares," she said, plopping into the god's lap, "what are you doing with these ridiculous creatures? Come with me to Persia. The food's better, and there's always a war on."

"In a moment, darling," Ares assured her, lifting her off his lap and slapping her generous fanny. "I want to have some fun with these mortals."

"What do you want with us?" asked Nicolaus. "Leave us alone!"

"I must tell your fortune." Ares arose from the table and spread wide his arms. "You will be consumed with hate. You will destroy one another, and the ground on which you fall will be cursed. Even the vultures that eat your flesh will be filled with a cancerous rage."

"How lovely!" exclaimed Enyo. "Wish we could stay and enjoy it, but we've better places to be."

"I curse you, as well!" Nicolaus shouted, jumping onto the table. "May you rot in the Underworld!"

'Rot?' Ares smiled, smugly. "I think not. I think that I shall never rot. You see, I'm too much in demand. The mobs clamor for me."

Long after Ares and his friends disappeared, their stench hung in the air. It was acrid and choking. Yet a far more lethal poison began to flow through the veins of the mortals. It was hate—the emotional hemlock—and it nearly brought them to ruin.

It first manifested in Ocyrrhoe, for Aphrodite had neglected to bind the young woman's heart to Telemus. She became cold and insolent towards her husband, and she scorned her marriage bed. She had an affair with a bodybuilder, and she diddled with a swarthy Persian slave. She even made passes at Nicolaus, which triggered her sister's wrath. Polyeuctus sided with Phobe; Hippodamia sided with Ocyrrhoe; and the slaves were divided in opinion between their master and mistress. Telemus blamed Nicolaus for tempting Ocyrrhoe, and Nicolaus accused Telemus of not being able to control his wife. This soup of ill will came to a boil one evening when a brawl broke out in the atrium. Spartan and Attican, man and woman, master and slave: all were bent on murder. Such was the scene when doves and a shower of rose petals signaled the return of Aphrodite.

"Look at you," she said, as they stood in shame before her. "Why did you capitulate before that fool Ares? Did you find my bliss insufficient? Was not your lot improved by love? Did you think to improve it with hatred?"

"Oh, superlative goddess, what weapons were we to use against Ares and his stinkers?" Polyeuctus asked. "Had we reason for hope? Could we have stood against a god?"

"You dared stand against me," Aphrodite reminded him. "And yes, you had every reason to hope. Love is the only weapon worth possessing, and I had amply armed you. Do you not yet comprehend? Through love, a man becomes a god; while a god, without love, is less than a man. You could have resisted Ares, you chose not to."

"What must we do to rekindle the love within us?" asked Nicolaus.

"If you think you have any love left in you, then feed it!" the goddess urged. "Feed it and tend it, as you would a choice vine. It will provide you with the fruit of peace and the wine of contentment."

It may seem implausible, but the fact is that those mortals followed her advice. They cultivated love and did so without any more help or hindrance from Mount Olympus. They fed one another nutritional compliments and watered with compassion. They weeded daily for envy and sarcasm and fertilized with humility. In time, those silly mortals became more admirable than any of their gods.

Chapter 3

GUNNHILD AND THE FROST GIANT

NUG IN THE REGION OF TRONDELAG, IN THE NORTH OF what is today known as Norway, the Viking jarldom of Upprike once flourished. It covered a vast area along the coast and encompassed eleven farms, but its principal port sat deep in the throat of the Trondheimsfjord. This was the hamlet of Urdastad.

Few places were as lovely as Urdastad. The receding tentacles of a glacier loomed above it, and waterfalls plunged from the high plateaus to the emerald-green fjord. In spring, the waters teemed with spawning salmon, and herring came late in the summer. On the steep mountain slopes, the dairymaids tended their cows, and the sheep and horses lazily grazed in the pastures. There were fields of rye, wheat, and oats; and the surrounding forests were home to reindeer, bear, and wild boar.

The pride of all Upprike was Urdastad's fleet of longboats, which protected the region and terrorized the rest of the known world. There were over forty vessels, most with fourteen pairs of oars. They were fantastic creations, made of oak, with red and white sails and dragon carvings. They plied not only the North, Baltic, and Irish Seas, but also the Rhine and Danube Rivers. Built for speed in raids and war, they were as vital for trade and whale hunting. Their sailors came from all around the region, for there was no shortage of men hell-bent for adventure.

A ring-fort defended the settlement from Danish raids. It was built of stone and timber and had but one gate. Reed-thatched, wooden houses sat within it, as did a firehouse and a well house.

Opposite the gate was the Great Hall. It was long and lofty, used both as a castle and as a meeting place for "The Thing," which was a sort of freeman council.

The jarl of Upprike was Olaf-the-Purple, so named because his passion for berries of any variety had permanently stained his teeth. In his youth, he had been a ruthless thug, renowned for his strength and sadism. By plunder, rape, and slaughter, he earned the respect of his people. He eventually slew and gutted the reigning jarl and took the office himself. This elevated status mellowed him considerably, and he married and took up gardening.

By middle age, Olaf-the-Purple had outlived three of his five wives and twelve of his thirteen children. His only surviving child was his daughter Gunnhild. He adored her, even though her long, blonde locks and big bones reminded him of her mother, who'd run off with a Frisian trader. He showered the girl with gifts of gold rings, necklaces, and torques and bragged about her fierce spirit.

When Gunnhild came of age, she fell in love with one of her father's bodyguards—a chap named Dag Treethighs. Her affection was returned and even surpassed. Olaf-the-Purple consented to their betrothal and promised a substantial dowry, on the condition that Dag proved his valor in the fleet's upcoming season of sacking. Dag agreed, and the deal was sealed with a bloodletting.

A nine-day feast commenced at the vernal equinox, and sacrifices were made to Odin, Thor, and Frey. Over fifty animals and eight Christian thralls were put to the knife in a sacred grove of evergreens. This was done to coax abundant crops, prosperous raids, and the safe return of the sailors.

There was a banquet held in the wide-gabled hall on the last night of sacrifices, and Gunnhild served at her father's table. She filled horns with ale, mead, and warm blood. She ladled skyr, or curdled milk, over bowls of porridge, and she set down trenchers of piping hot horse-flesh and plump, purple whale steaks. Each time she came to Dag's seat, he winked and tugged on her braids. When the jugglers began performing, Dag seized the moment and pulled her into a dark corner.

"My golden apples!" he gasped, in the old, Norse tongue, as he pressed his head to her breasts.

"They are yours," she promised. "They will always be yours until Ragnarok, the day of doom."

"Don't be gloomy, for tomorrow I sail for Semgallen." Dag tossed his red hair out of his face and pinned Gunnhild to the wall. "Oh, that I could taste the honeyed fruit before me!"

"Not without earning it, as father has told thee," Gunnhild reminded him. "Return to me before the first snowfall, hero, with scars and plenty of loot. I will be worth the trouble."

So Dag sailed off to adventure, and Gunnhild waited at home, preparing her trousseau. The days passed. The Scandinavian summer, with its foggy days and short nights, gave way to autumn chill. The snows arrived, but Dag did not.

That winter brought much hardship and death to Urdastad. It was so cold that the old, dying glacier expanded, and the Trondheimsfjord became a solid sheet of ice. The reed-thatched roofs sagged under the weight of the snow, and many houses caved in from the heavy drifts. Livestock froze; food became scarce; and people began to perish. It kept snowing and snowing, day after day, and the wind never ceased to howl.

The elders of "The Thing" met with Olaf-the-Purple to see what, if anything, could be done about this catastrophe. They concluded that they were being punished by the gods and that some supreme offering was wanted. With tears in his eyes, Olaf agreed to sacrifice his only child on the Winter Solstice.

When Gunnhild was told of her impending death, she didn't bat an eyelash. She was sorely disappointed by Dag's evident failure, and she no longer cared to live. She rose early on the appointed day and put on a sky-blue gown, a sable coat, and a golden headdress. With gusto, she trudged through the drifts to the grove of evergreens and laid herself upon the runestone altar.

Olaf-the-Purple was overcome with grief, and had to be helped to the altar. He burst into sobs and thrice dropped the knife. Finally, he gripped it in both hands and raised it high above his head. Before he could plunge it into Gunnhild, the stone beneath her began to speak.

"Hold!" boomed the stone, who was really the god Odin in disguise. "Lay not a hand on thy daughter!"

"Why not?" asked Gunnhild, exasperated.

"Because I said so!" the stone answered, trembling with indignation. "Throw down the knife, Olaf!"

The jarl did so, and the elders swarmed him and began to shout in his ears. "Ask the stone what it wants!" insisted one, while another fellow screamed, "I'm cold!" They made such a racket that Olaf-the-Purple couldn't think. Then an earth tremor threw them to their knees, and they got quiet after that.

"What do the gods of Asgard demand?" Olaf-the-Purple asked the stone. "What must we do to appease them?"

"It is not the gods who have brought on thy troubles," replied the stone, "but the giants. There is a Frost Giant in Jotunheim named Ulf. It is he that has blown you this foul winter, for he wants to destroy you."

"Why should he?" inquired Olaf-the-Purple. "What have we ever done to him?"

"You have prospered; that is enough."

"I don't like the sound of this Frost Giant." Olaf-the-Purple folded his arms and snorted with consternation. "What are we to do about him?"

"If you want to survive, you'll have to go to Jutenheim and slay him," said the stone. "But be careful, because he likes to bite off heads."

"Which one of us can do battle with a giant?" The jarl looked around at the pitiful assembly. "Alas, our young men are lost at sea, and we are old and weak with hunger."

"Let me go, Father!" begged Gunnhild. "Let me be the one to go and—"

"Never!" declared Olaf-the Purple. "I cannot send a woman to do a man's job."

"Excuse me?" Gunnhild put her fists on her wide hips. "Uh, I believe that I am better with a sword than you, and no man in Trondelag can match me with a battle-ax. Why, I could split that tree in half, standing from here. I'm young and strong as an ox. Let me at this Ulf! I'll carve the blood-eagle on his back!"

"Calm down," cooed Olaf-the Purple, as he tried, in vain, to restrain her. "I cannot spare you, daughter."

"A moment ago, you were going to slice me up," she reminded him. "This way, at least, I can be of real use."

"She's got a point," said the stone. "I wouldn't want her taking an ax to me.'

"Oh, all right," Olaf-the-Purple relented. "But I insist on an escort. She's a virgin, you know."

"Father!"

"Not a problem," the stone assured him. "She can take some thralls, and to their number she shall add the earth-spirit Loki. He knows the way to Jotunheim, for he's the son of a giant."

"Loki?" Olaf-the-Purple was stunned. "Loki, the trickster? Can he be trusted with my daughter?"

"He can't be trusted with anyone or anything," admitted the stone, "but you have no say in the matter."

The folk of Urdastad rounded up two skinny horses that had not yet been put in a stew. They hooked them to a sleigh packed with blankets, dried fish, and terrified thralls. As the torchbearers held the crowd back, Gunnhild emerged from the Great Hall. She wore a whalebone corset and a bronze breastplate beneath a practical bearskin coat. On her head sat a cone-shaped, leather helmet, complete with nose guard. A sword swung from her hip; a spear pulsed in her hand; and a circular shield was strapped to her back. She was ready for action and ready for speed, and she threw all but one of the English thralls from her sleigh to lighten her load. She then took the reins and called for the earth-spirit Loki.

Loki sprang from the shadows and onto the sleigh. He was lanky but attractive, with dimples and the eyes of a wolf. He was a libertine, and his lips curled as he slipped a long arm around Gunnhild's waist and roughly pulled her to him.

"Let's get started, shall we?" she asked, jabbing her elbow into his ribs. "Oops, I didn't realize you were sitting so close. You'd better scoot over since, I confess, I ate a chunk of gammelost for supper."

She let out a piercing whistle to spur the horses. They didn't budge; they thought it cruel, indeed, to be pressed into service when they'd already resigned themselves to death from starvation. Gunnhild persisted. She thrashed them with her whip and screamed insults, but the most she got from them was a couple of heavy sighs. Finally, Loki threw back his head, and a wolf-like howl escaped from deep within his long, slender throat. The villagers waved good-bye as the sleigh tore off across the snow and up the mountain.

Gunnhild, Loki, and the one English thrall made strange traveling companions. The thrall sang hymn after hymn, until Gunnhild turned around and boxed his ears. Then Loki transformed himself into a mirror image of Gunnhild and tried to wrestle away the reins. The sleigh nearly went off a precipice and into a crevasse before Loki returned to his own body and laughingly surrendered.

A fortnight later, he shape-changed again—this time into Dag Treethighs. Despite attempts to restrain herself, Gunnhild was overcome with lust. She threw herself into his lap and began to suck on his lips. But when she looked up into the wolfish eyes, she was wracked with revulsion. She slapped Loki so hard that one of his teeth cracked, and she lost her meager breakfast in the snow.

After crossing the frozen river Glivagar, they entered Jotunheim, the land of the giants. Everything was large—which is perhaps not so surprising. The snowflakes were as large as meat platters, and the ice-covered trees were as tall as mountains. The thrall fainted the first time he saw a giant's footprint, and even stalwart Gunnhild hesitated before the drawbridge to Ulf's castle.

This titanic residence was completely crafted from ice. Its rectangular shape, proportions, and many gables were Scandinavian, in design; but the twin, squat towers—a recent addition—were unmistakably Germanic. The gate was raised, and two guards were positioned beneath it. They were intensely ugly giants, each more than a hundred feet tall.

"How are we to get past them?" Gunnhild asked Loki.

"Don't sweat it," the earth spirit told her. "Ulf is my second cousin, once removed. I'll claim the thrall as my own property, but what shall we do with you? Ulf is a confirmed bachelor; he doesn't get on with pushy women."

"Hey!"

"Oh, come on," Loki said. "You're not exactly a withering rose, dearie. I know, we'll pass you off as...as an elf."

It took them all the afternoon to cross the drawbridge, and, by then, the guards changed. The new ones seemed jolly enough. They recognized Loki and warmly greeted him, once he'd gained their attention by setting their boots on fire. One of the guards cupped the three travelers in his palm, placed them on his shoulder, and took them to Ulf.

"Well, Loki!" bellowed the Frost Giant, who sat drinking ale from the inverted dome of a Byzantine basilica. "Long time, no see!"

"It has been some time, cousin," agreed Loki. "Sorry I didn't get around to answering any of your letters. You know how it is. Busy and what-not."

"Yes," Ulf said, "I imagine it must get mighty busy up in Asgard with the gods.'

"Well, I...uh..."

"Where did we go wrong with you, Loki?"

"Huh?"

"Was it because your mother was alien?"

"Now, watch it, cousin..."

"What possessed you to abandon us giants in favor of those inferior gods, hmm?"

"Is this a bad time?" Loki asked. "Because I can always stay over at Aunt Angerbode's."

"Ah, sit down and be still," grumbled Ulf. "I'm just messing with you. Pour some ale for yourself and your little pals, there."

"Thanks," squeaked the thrall. "Got cheese?"

That night, they glutted on ribs the size of longboats, and raw oysters as big as octopuses. Throughout the meal, Ulf repeatedly left the table to kick his jester. Each time he did so, Loki poured a powerful sedative into Ulf's dome of ale. The Frost Giant was soon slurring his words, and his eyes grew heavy.

"The problem with the gods is that th-th-they don't want to work for a living," Ulf complained, while the wheel-size, ligonberry tarts were being served. "They're lazy, and th-th-that's why we will ultimately defeat them. And the mortals are even worse. They're taking over Scandinavia!"

"Hm," Loki commented, noncommittally.

"T-t-too darn lazy!" stressed Ulf. "And my own kinsman soils himself in their company!"

"Rather a poor choice of words, wouldn't you say, cousin?"

But Ulf said no more. He passed out and fell from his chair with a great thud. The three travelers shredded their napkins and made a rope, by which they repelled from the table. Gunnhild drew her sword, preparing to stab the Frost Giant, but Loki stopped her.

"What are you doing?" he asked.

"I'm going to carve the blood-eagle on his back, like I said I would," Gunnhild answered. "Why?"

"Aw, that'll take forever, and he might awaken," said Loki. "Let's just find a kitchen cleaver, and the three of us can chop off his head."

"I say, what a cleaver idea!" punned the thrall. "The sooner we exit this place, the better!"

So they took off Ulf's head and rolled it into the fire. They then fled through the cavernous halls, careful to avoid the many servants. They rejoiced when they reached the gate, but Ulf's giant cat blocked their escape.

"Trrrrrr," the cat purred. "What have we here? An earth-spirit, an elf, and a mortal. Mmmm. I like variety."

"We didn't come here to slay felines," Gunnhild said.

"No, you came to kill off my easy source of food!" snapped the cat. "I'm used to roe and lutefisk. What am I supposed to do now—go through the trash ditch?"

"Here," Loki said, pushing the thrall forward. "Eat this fellow and let the elf and me pass.'

"Wait!" protested the thrall. "I'm old, pussy! I'd be tough meat!"

"Hardly worth my trouble," agreed the cat. "No, I think I'm in the mood for some elf."

Loki had no regard for any mortal, but he knew Odin would be angry if Gunnhild perished. With a world-weary sigh, the earth-spirit shape-changed into a giant elkhound. He said "woof," and the cat jumped from all fours straight into the rafters. Then Gunnhild and the thrall climbed onto Loki's back, and he ran past the guards and down the drawbridge to the sleigh.

"Hurry up and jump in!" Gunnhild shouted to Loki, when he'd

returned to his own body. "Aren't you coming with us?"

"I don't believe I am," Loki told her. "I think, now I'm here, I may as well look in on Aunt Angerbode. Never know when I'll be back this way. You go home. You'll be fine. Only, look out for the fierce snow tiger, because he's fond of Viking women. Just kidding. There are no tigers in Scandinavia."

"Whatever," said Gunnhild, impatiently.

She cracked her whip, and the scrawny horses looked back at her in horror. They stumbled about, foamed at the mouth, and moaned. So Loki used his magic once more, and transformed the pathetic creatures into vigorous stallions. They bucked, then sped away, and the sleigh soon passed out of Jotunheim.

Upon her return to Urdastad, Gunnhild found her beloved village restored to summer glory. The cowbells tinkled from the dark green slopes, and the tette bloomed in the meadows. The cuckoos sang from the mountain ash trees, and the lambs skipped across the pastures. Best of all, the fjord had thawed and was bright with red-and-white sails. The fleet had come home!

She abandoned her sleigh at the snow line and ran down the mountain as fast as she could. Olaf-the-Purple embraced her, and the villagers called her a heroine and lifted her onto their shoulders. They gave her a horn of mead and put a wreath of flowers on her head.

When her eyes met Dag's, she was moved beyond words and relieved to find him scarred and rich. They were married soon after, in a marvelous ceremony, and the skalds composed odes in their honor. They were so happy, in fact, that to show their appreciation, they sacrificed the English thrall to Odin.

Chapter 4

N'GAMO AND
THE WITCH DOCTOR

N THE HIGH JUNGLES OF THE CONGO—LONG BEFORE THE Portuguese, French, Belgians, or Henry Stanley came calling—there lived a tribe of pygmies who had never seen a white man. They slept in rounded huts made of twigs and banana leaves. They ate fresh fruit, roasted huge spiders, and hunted a variety of game. They navigated their rivers in dugouts, and painted their bodies with pigments extracted from berries, grasses, and earth. Their chief joy was making music— rhythmic creations that accompanied their daily activities and heightened to frenzy at full moons, marriages, and funerals. During times of war the drums became especially active, for the pygmies had no written language and did not feel the need for one.

The war drums were busy that sultry afternoon when the young widow Bouhaweh gave birth to her only child—a son she named N'gamo. He was a puny baby—scarcely bigger than a fat banana—and the midwives doubted he would survive in the dangerous forest world they inhabited. But Bouhaweh determined her son would survive. He was all she had left of her husband Songdu, who'd taken a poison dart in the neck. So she nursed N'gamo and prayed to Hashgow-e, the millipede god, that the child might live.

N'gamo not only survived, he thrived. He grew strong in limb, fleet of foot, and sharp of mind. He excelled at hunting and fishing and was the best of his generation at war games. He knew the jungle like the back of his hand and made awesome speed through the dense bush without snapping a twig or stepping on a scorpion. N'gamo would have been a natural-born leader—possibly chief of his tribe someday—but for one thing: he possessed no musical gifts whatsoever.

The elders tried their best to remedy this retardation. Time and again, they attempted to instruct him upon the drums, but were brought to frustration by his sluggish, faltering fingers. True, his singing voice was powerful...and also nasal, strained, and habitually flat. Worse still, he couldn't dance. When he tried, he suffered humiliation and significant bruising.

These were serious flaws, and the people were puzzled. After all, Songdu had been a talented drummer, and Bouhaweh was known for her thrilling tongue-trilling. Maybe, the villagers thought, the lad was cursed, and Hashgow-e had denied him the ecstasy of music and dance. They grew suspicious of N'gamo and shunned him. He was no longer welcomed on hunting parties, and the pretty girls pointed at him and snickered.

N'gamo grew miserable, feeling he had shamed his mother and the memory of his father. When he turned sixteen, he left the village. He embraced his mother and asked her to remember him.

"I won't return," he told her, "until I drum like rain, sing like bird, and dance like fire."

As Bouhaweh wept on the bank of the Congo, N'gamo rowed his dugout away from all he knew. After two days on the river, he set off on foot across the densely forested mountains. There, where the leaves were always moist with mist and the air was thin and perfumed with decomposition, N'gamo made a home for himself. He built a hut, gathered roots and berries, and fished a nearby stream.

He did have neighbors, of a sort. A family of gorillas lived near, and he often caught them spying on him. A leopard also stalked him, so that he had to keep embers burning throughout the nights to serve as a deterrent. As far as he could tell, he was the only human in the area.

To keep from dwelling on memories of home, he kept busy with chores. He also spent a lot of time practicing his drumming, singing, and dancing. His fingers hardly rested, and he regularly belted out the songs of his tribe across the Great Rift Valley. He rehearsed all the dance steps he'd been taught, until his muscles burned and throbbed. Despite these efforts, his performance showed no signs of improvement.

The years passed, and N'gamo's life developed a comforting routine. But his peace was shattered at dawn one morning, when he was jolted awake by a high-pitched squeal that seemed otherworldly. He opened his eyes to find a creature squatting beside him. It had foul breath, raging eyes, and a surplus of tattoos, piercings, and facial mutilations. Its chest was bare and drooping, and its skirt was made of shrunken heads.

"Aiiiii!" screamed N'gamo.

"Aiiiii!" screamed the creature.

"Get off me, you demon!"

"I'm no demon," the creature said, "and I'm not on you, but beside you." It shifted its fat, squatting frame from knee to knee, causing the shrunken heads to knock against the earthen floor of the hut. "I am Naka-Lot the witch doctor."

"So?" Now that N'gamo knew it was a man beside him—and a silly looking one, at that—his courage mustered to the point of arrogance. "I don't need a witch doctor. I did not send for one; I did not wish for one; and I am not pleased to see one in my hut. Remove yourself from my mountain!"

"This isn't your mountain," said Naka-lot. "This mountain belongs to itself."

"No, it doesn't," N'gamo insisted. "It belongs to me, because I'm the strongest man around. Ha-ha!"

"Yes, strong in body," agreed Naka-lot, "and strong in foolishness, too." He sat down, for his knees were cracking louder than the shrunken heads. "You need a witch doctor, sonny, because it's going to take magic to get you drumming, singing, and dancing."

"Huh?" N'gamo was again frightened. "How did you know I couldn't drum, sing, or dance?"

"The gorillas told me," replied Naka-lot, flipping his ocherdressed dreadlocks out of his face. "But you mustn't blame them, because your artistic incompetence is known by all the valley. You're so selfish you don't even think to spare the ears and eyes of your fellow creatures."

"You speak to the animals?"

"You don't?"

"No."

"Well, see, that's 'cause you're stupid," Naka-lot told him. "Don't you know that all of creation is talking, singing, or screaming? Doesn't the whistle of the wind affect you? Don't you fret a little when you hear it? Doesn't thunder startle you? Don't you sometimes think you've heard a bird call your name? Let me tell you something: a bird HAS called your name. She would tell you more, if you would but listen."

"One might imagine a bird has said anything," scoffed N'gamo. "One might go mad with imaginings."

"One might go mad without them. You can't let your fear of looking stupid stop you, because you'll look stupid if you do. You want to sing like bird? Great! Choose a bird, listen to what it says, and follow its advice. You want to drum like rain? Sounds grand, but get out in the rain and feel it drum against your body. You want to dance like fire? Okay, but that's a tough one. Some folks spend their whole lives making a study of fire. It takes patience. Look, even if you do everything I tell you, you're not going to be a musical genius; but you'll be in love with rhythm, melody, and grace, and that will make all the difference!"

Having said all he came to say, Naka-Lot waddled off into the jungle. His shrunken heads jostled, causing them to swing through the air and slam into tree trunks. N'gamo was alone again, but he wasted no time in idleness.

For the next few days, N'gamo labored to build up a supply of meat and fish, and he buried this bounty deep in the earth to preserve it. He gathered vegetables and fruit to dry in the sun, and stacked a big pile of firewood. Then, secure in his rations, he sat down to observe the birds.

There were countless types of birds in the Great Rift Valley: quacking ducks; elegant storks; vultures with warts; and pelicans with sagging gullets—to name a few. These birds were not known for their music, however, and N'gamo could not distinguish one songbird from another, since they all sang at the same time. In the end, a pigeon chose him.

"N'gamo!" the pigeon called one afternoon. "N'gamo!"

"Yes?" N'gamo answered, with great excitement. "I am here! I am here!"

"May I—ooo—perch on—ooo—your arm?"

"Sure, go ahead," said N'gamo, crooking his elbow.

"Ooo—ooo!" exclaimed the pigeon, breathily, as she fluttered down from a giant lobelia and bounced to a landing. "Aw, crap! I think I've put on weight again."

"Too many berries?"

"Nah, it's those darn worms that put it on me." She stuck out her talon to shake. "The name's Phyllis."

"Phyllis?" N'gamo scrunched up his face. "That's weird!"

"Yeah, I know," agreed Phyllis, rolling her beady eyes. "I get teased a lot about it, but that's my real name. My folks were from up north. Listen, I'm going to teach you to sing—specifically, how to coo."

And she did. Before long, N'gamo mastered his scales; and he sang from his diaphragm, rather than through his nose. He relaxed his throat, and focused on coming down on top of a pitch to correct his tendency to flatten. He sang so well that the songbirds sang along with him, and elephants tapped their feet and swung their trunks. The snakes rose up on their tails, bobbed and grinned. The leopard purred and boogied...well, suffice it to say that N'gamo could sing.

He next turned his attention to drumming. Whenever it rained—and it rains rather a lot in a tropical rain forest—N'gamo stripped himself of his loin cloth and stood, naked, to let the drops drum against him. Sometimes, they pelted and stung; but more often, they trickled, tickled, and pleased. He came to understand rhythm's effect on his emotions, and he was soon drumming like the rain.

"Now," he said to himself, "I will learn to dance like fire."

He constructed a bonfire and sat cross-legged before it. He studied the licking flames and popping sparks. Hour upon hour, day after day, he continued his observations until his supply of firewood was exhausted. He collected more logs; these, too, became ashes; and still, N'gamo felt he had learned nothing about dance. Then his eyes caught sight of the smoking volcano on the horizon.

'Yes,' he thought, 'I will travel to the lava flows, for they are an endless source of fire.'

Taking only his courage, he ran through the forest, down the mountain, across the valley, and up the side of the volcano. He had to cross a section of crust to get to the lava flows. The crust varied in its thickness and was not as sturdy as it looked. N'gamo knew he could fall through and be instantly cremated by the molted lava, which ran beneath the surface. He was determined, nevertheless, and stepped out onto the crust.

His feet began to burn, at once, so he had to step quickly. His knees jerked up and down; his elbows poked to the sides; and his toes flexed. His hips swayed from side to side, and his pelvis thrust to and fro. His head wagged; his shoulders shimmied; and his torso twisted.

"I'm dancing!" he cried, rejoicing. "I'm dancing!"

Later, when N'gamo was cooling his heels in the Congo, Naka-Lot appeared from the jungle. The witch doctor was in a good mood. He laughed so hard that his shrunken heads seemed to laugh along as they rode the waves of his fat.

"N'gamo, you are something ELSE!" he declared, when he'd caught sufficient breath. "Talking to pigeons; standing in the rain; and walking on the ceiling of oblivion!"

"So what?" N'gamo smiled right back at him. "I don't regret any of it. In fact, I must thank you, Naka-Lot, for you changed my life. I can now drum like rain, sing like bird, and dance like fire! I can return to my tribe and take my rightful place among them! I can make my mother proud of me!"

"Yes, yes," agreed Naka-Lot, with a wink, "and you may have your pick of brides, too. But, you know, sonny, I'm afraid you'll never be able to paint."

Chapter 5

GIULIA AND THE ANGEL

IOVANNI TORNACANTE—A FILTHY-RICH BANKER, HACK poet, and pal of Lorenzo de'Medici—was, first and foremost, the patriarch of one of the most powerful houses in Florence. Shrewd and ruthless, he advanced his family at every opportunity. Where there was no opportunity, he did not shrink from creating one. He protected his kinsmen and made certain that even the most useless and infirm among them had every creature comfort...so long as they kept their mouths shut.

But woe to any Tornacantes who dared plot against him! More than one of them were found strangled in their beds or floating in the Arno. Giovanni's own mother, foiled in her attempt to bludgeon her son, was dispatched by a viper hidden in her sewing box.

In spite of these unsavory facts—or perhaps because of them—Giovanni was a Laurentian celebrity. He dominated the Ghilbelline Party and was a generous benefactor to the Dominicans. His bawdy verse was popular with the lascivious, and his mistresses were plump and clever. A humanist, his zest for art was so great that he murdered one young painter to increase the market value of his collection.

But more than his power, palazzi, and paintings, Giovanni prized his daughter Giulia. She was nothing like him. He and his sons were dark in features and thoughts, but Giulia was fair in every way.

"Pura siccome un angelo, Iddio mi die' una figlia!" he often said to his friends; which means, "God gave me a daughter as pure as an angel!"

In truth, Guilia Tornacante was amazingly innocent. She was

kept in luxurious seclusion, spending her hours in the company of women. Her mother and aunts—lovely ladies, but self-absorbed—spoke only of fashion, lovers, and intrigue. Her duenna Maddalena was a bully, and her female cousins were insipid. As for the nuns who lurked in the shadows, Giulia thought them sweet, but dull.

She did spend time with her father, of course, and her brothers Giorgio and Ridolfo. She was also occasionally allowed to mix with her male cousins on feast days or at weddings and funerals, though never without Maddalena at her side. She certainly got her fill of clergymen; but all in all, she felt deprived of secular, male companionship.

This began to change when Giulia turned fifteen. As word spread of her beauty, the rush was on to possess her. Nearly every day, aristocratic suitors arrived at the Palazzo Tornacante, and Guilia was paraded out for them in pink cloth and pearls. By spring, it seemed as though all the males in Northern Italy were lining up at the gates in hopes of gaining an audience. It was then decided that the Tornacantes would flee to the refuge of their summer villa to gain some measure of peace.

The day prior to the family's departure was an eventful one in the life of Florence. It began calmly enough for Guilia, with a mass in the Tornacante chapel and a breakfast in the garden. When she returned to her bedchamber—a cool, elegant room that overlooked the Via Maggio—she began to oversee the packing of her summer dresses, her ribbons, and her wide-brimmed paglia. She had moved on to the storage of her winter garments when chaos erupted in the street. She ran to a window and threw open the shutters.

The crowds below were frenetic, running in every direction. Women were screaming, and men were tussling. Guilia's brothers Giorgio and Ridolfo were muscling their way down the Via Maggio with a gang of their kinsmen, their foils banging against their swaggering hips. When they entered the Palazzo Tornacante, a commotion ensued. Hurried footsteps echoed down the halls, and masculine commands rang out from the lower chambers. Guilia begged to go and investigate, but Maddalena insisted they stay put. At length, all members of the family were summoned to the courtyard, where Giovanni addressed them.

"You know too well that the Pazzi's are our sworn enemies," he told them. "For many years, they attempted to mask their treachery with smiles and flattery. Today, they removed those masks!"

Giovanni went on to explain that, while at mass with the Medici in the Cathedral of Santa Maria del Fiore, Pazzi assassins drew their daggers and struck down Lorenzo's brother, Giuliano. Lorenzo, himself, was wounded but escaped to safety. This heinous deed appeared to be the fruition of a widespread conspiracy, said to include an archbishop and even the Papal Father. But the truehearted Florentines were falling in behind Lorenzo, and the assassins were sure to taste death before nightfall.

"I swear, we are already hanging Pazzi pigs from the windows of the Palazzo della Signoria," Giorgio boasted, to reassure the ladies. "I, myself, killed plenty of Pazzi today; and Ridolfo here killed at least one. We are now going back to kill more Pazzi. Go to your rooms and see that your doors are barred. By tomorrow, this will be finished. Then, we will have a nice summer at the villa, eh?"

"Papa," Guilia pleaded, while the family dispersed, "may I spend this confinement alone, without the servants, nuns, or..."

"Or your duenna?"

"Si," admitted Guilia. "I can't help it Papa. It's how I feel. Maddalena will insist on tedious conversation, and I prefer to rest before our journey."

"The journey must be postponed!" Giovanni told her, wringing his hands with anticipation. "This is no time to be off chasing butterflies in the country, my girl! Don't you understand what has happened? The citizens of Florence love their Lorenzo more than ever. They are calling him 'Il Magnifico'! Ha! They'll give him whatever he wants now. Well, by all things sacred, the Tornacantes will be there, by his side! That includes you, so I hope you haven't yet packed your prettiest dress."

"If I'm to dance tomorrow, that's all the more reason to rest today," Guilia sweetly said, as she smiled up at her father. "I wish you would give me a moment away from Maddalena, Papa."

"Oh, very well," Giovanni acquiesced. He, too, thought the duenna was a terrible bore, and he had contemplated her murder upon a number of occasions. "But I shall have a guard posted outside your door, in case there's any trouble."

When Guilia was locked into her bedchamber, she giddily removed her sleeves. She opened her shutters, leaned over the Via Maggio, and was held, rapt, by the continuing action. A gang, wearing the colors of the House of Nori, galloped up on their powerful steeds and halted before the Palazzo Tornacante.

"Have you been long at that window, Signorina?" one of the Nori horsemen called up to Guilia. "Have you seen a Pazzi run by? A young man, dressed in black?"

"I've seen no Pazzis," Guilia answered, haughtily. "We are boarded up here." An urge to brag suddenly overtook her. "My brothers Giorgio and Ridolfo have killed many Pazzis today."

"Ah, you must be the famous Guilia!" exclaimed the same horseman, doffing his cap and bowing from his saddle. "Si, Giorgio is a useful man. We are seeking to avenge our cousin Francesco. He was butchered alongside Giuliano de'Medici. We are hunting down that knave Marco Pazzi. He has twice been banished from the city, but he will never learn until we cut his throat. Buena Sera, Signorina!"

The Nori horsemen rode off, and Guilia left the window and went into her prayer closet. She lit a votive, and, as Giorgio had requested, she made prayers for her kinsmen. She prayed they would return alive and victorious. She asked this, aloud, many times; and she silently repeated it, as her slender fingers caressed her rosary beads.

After an hour of pious devotion, her mind began to wander. She recalled the faces of many of her suitors. Some of them were from the best families, some handsome, some young, some devout, and some were rich; but none of them were all of these things. She wondered which of them her father would choose, and she hoped he would discount them all.

"Oh, You Hosts of Heaven!" she prayed. "Please send me a suitor I can love. A handsome man if possible. A man who will respect the bonds of parentado."

She had scarcely spoken these words when an angel appeared. It was a marvelous being, of surpassing beauty, with androgynous features and a milk-and-peaches complexion. It was adorned in snowy-white raiment and had great wings that majestically pulsed to keep it bobbing aloft the prie-dieu.

"Guilia," it said in a voice that was as many voices, "do you know what you are asking?"

"What I am asking?" repeated Guilia, who had gone whey-faced with shock. "Why, I—I suppose I'm asking for love."

"Poor child!" the angel gasped, crossing itself. "Love is a dangerous gift—an expensive one, too. Wouldn't you rather marry an elderly, rich man who would give you little trouble and leave you in peace?"

"No, I would not," answered Guilia, recovering her wits. "Who are you, anyway?"

"Didn't I say?" The angel covered its mouth and tittered. "I am your guardian angel Tullioa."

"How do you do?" Guilia stood and curtsied. "Are you here to help find me a suitable husband?"

"Forgive me, my dear, but you were not praying for a suitable husband. You were praying for love, and that's quite another thing."

"Is it?" Guilia asked. "Only a man I love could be a suitable husband."

"Oh, drat these new-fangled, Renaissance sensibilities!" complained Tullioa. "It used to be so easy in the Dark Ages. Humans used to content themselves with fuel, oats, and salvation. Now, the only thing that girls pray for is love, love, love! It will be the end of civilization—mark my words! I've seen it happen, time and time again. Hob-nail boots climbing up the ladder, and silver slippers sliding down the other side."

"You're not at all like what I imagined an angel to be."

"Is that so?" Tullioa irritably waved away a stray feather. "I wouldn't throw stones, Guilia. Oh, I know everybody goes on and on about your sensational innocence, but don't forget that I'm your guardian angel. I've been running about in that head of yours for fifteen years. I well remember the time you stuck out your tongue at that statue of Saint Eusebius, and I also recall a certain wink you gave Monsignor Rucellai."

"That was an innocent wink!"

"No wink is innocent, child. It denotes conspiracy or lust, and usually both in this town. Nevertheless, I perceive that you are spoiled, and it really may take love to break you. So be it. But I want it understood, from the first, that I am not liable—not even if you're a casualty."

"I understand," said Guilia. "When may I have my love?"

"Foolish girl!" Tullioa scolded. "You shall have your love this very night!"

In a flash, Tullioa disappeared; and Guilia tried to make sense of it all. She considered the angel's last words preposterous. How would a lover find her now, when she was locked in her bedchamber with a guard at the door? Perhaps her guardian angel had faulty, precognitive skills—or else could perform miracles.

She left her prayer closet and stood for a time at her window. The setting sun banished the proud towers of Florence to silhouette and abandoned the Via Maggio to shadow. Something was amiss in the twilight. Guilia could not pinpoint the source of her uneasiness, but she knew she shared the anxiety of the citizens who furtively rushed to the safety of their homes.

The April night thickened, and she grew chilly. She closed the shutters, then slipped into a liberating nightdress. She dipped a linen towel into a bowl of water and removed the day's dust from her face, neck, cleavage, and legs. She had moved on to her toes, when a maid brought in a tray of cheese, bread, and fruit and locked the door behind her as she left. Guilia ignored the tray, said a brief prayer, and pulled back her bed curtains—to find a man in her bed!

She wanted to scream—heaven knows, she tried—but not a sound would escape her throat. She wanted to flee but found she could not. She stood there, more dumbstruck than she'd been over Tullioa. She could only quiver, as the man—whose black doublet was open, exposing his moist, hairy chest—slowly took the lamp from her hand and set it on a stand. He sat her down on the bed, gently, and pressed his lips to her ear.

"I do not want to harm you, Signorina," he whispered, "so do not try to sound the alarm. I am not afraid to die, but I admit, I'm in no hurry."

"I do not desire your death, Signor," Guilia managed to say, as she took in his dark, curly locks; his bold nose and lips; and his eyes, which reflected the lamplight.

"That is because you do not know who I am."

"You are the assassin Marco Pazzi, no?"

"I am!" he cried, standing to thump his fist against his chest. "I had no idea my notoriety had spread to such a degree."

"Some Noris rode by and told me of you," explained Guilia. "They intend to cut your throat."

"My throat?" Marco gulped, then struck his chest again. "Let the dogs try!"

"How did you get in my room?"

"Eh, I can scale any wall. You were in your prayer closet, being a good daughter to your pig of a father."

"My father is a man of great achievement!"

"Your father, Guilia, is a ghoul from hell, and all of Florence knows it." Marco chose an apple from the tray, tossed it in the air a

47

couple of times, and then sank his teeth into it. "You see, I know who you are, as well. Your name is as notorious as mine. You are Guilia Tornacante—the harlot who will be sold to the highest bidder."

"How dare you!"

Guilia lunged at him, but he caught her and embraced her. She beat against his chest, but he kissed her, hard, on the lips until her arms went limp by her side. He carried her to the bed and threw her upon it. But then, a seizure of shame racked him. He buried his face in his hands and fled to a corner of the room.

"What?" demanded Guilia, sitting up on the bed. "Did I do something wrong?"

"Si," he said, weeping. "You should not have been willing, Signorina, but I was even more wrong to tempt you. We mustn't behave like the Medici. They are beasts; we are not."

This passion, followed by disgust, established a pattern that lasted through the night. Lust flared up between them like a rogue forest fire, then one of them doused it with a splash of guilty conscience. One moment, they were kissing; the next, they were on their knees praying. They could not deny their love, but they could not deny the wrongfulness of their position, either. After hours of this wrestling, peace was granted them. Dawn found them happily sleeping; their bodies intertwined.

The following evening, Filippo Bardi—a monk from the monastery of San Marco—moved through the halls of the Palazzo Tornacante. It was not unusual to find Dominicans within Giovanni's walls, for he was one of their richest patrons. But this monk was different.

His appearance was unsettling. He had sunken jowls, heavy eyebrows, and an eagle nose that hung over a protruding lower lip. His eyes were dialated and hyper-alert, suggesting the zeal of a fanatic.

48

Indeed, Brother Filippo was fanatical. He was convinced he knew all the answers worth knowing and that he was a chosen messenger of heaven. His self-deluding convictions made him enemies within the clergy, but also gained him a reputation as an expert inquisitor. He could extract the truth—never mind the means—from any reluctant witness. It was this "gift" for discovery that made him popular with the ruthless lords of Florence.

He cut through the courtyard and exited the palazzo, stopping outside the gate, where the Tornacante guards warmed themselves around a fire. At length, Giovanni, Giorgio, and Ridolfo joined him. Behind them, two ruffians bore the body of Marco Pazzi in a sack.

"I'm sure they must be doing something with all these Pazzi corpses," Giovanni said to Brother Filippo. "There must be a mass grave somewhere. Of course, there's the Pazzi Chapel. Si, my sons will dump him there. What of Guilia? You've spoken to her?"

"She knows nothing of Marco's death," Brother Filippo told him. "She thinks you will be merciful and allow them to marry."

"Then she is unrepentant?" Giovanni asked, disbelieving.

"She made her confession and withheld nothing," the monk said, rubbing his hands to warm them. "There was grave misconduct on her part, but I do not believe she was compromised. She still professes love for him, however, and at times she seems quite mad. She persists in some notion that she was visited by her guardian angel, and that this angel prophesied the coming of Marco."

"Stop!" Giovanni shouted, putting his hands over his ears. "Tell me no more!"

"You know what must be done, Papa!" urged Giorgio. "It may not be Guilia's fault, but she is damaged. She is no longer ours."

"You are so anxious to have a dead sister?" Giovanni asked, grabbing his eldest son by his shoulders.

"My sister is already dead!"

"Si, si," agreed Giovanni. "Then go up and do it yourself, but make it clean and quick."

49

"Of course."

"And Giorgio..."

"Si, Papa?"

"Tell her I love her."

Giorgio found his sister at prayer, and she ran into his arms and kissed him. She begged him to support her marriage to Marco, and Giorgio promised he would. She seemed so beautiful, so hopeful, so full of life. And then she was dead, and Tullioa collected her soul and lovingly carried her to Paradise.

Chapter 6

HAN AND
THE GOLDEN DRAGON

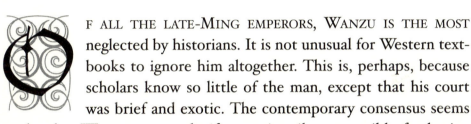

F ALL THE LATE-MING EMPERORS, WANZU IS THE MOST neglected by historians. It is not unusual for Western textbooks to ignore him altogether. This is, perhaps, because scholars know so little of the man, except that his court was brief and exotic. The contemporary consensus seems to be that Wanzu was partly, if not primarily, responsible for letting more power slip into the hands of the palace eunuchs. Obsessed with the minutest detail of their bureaucracy, the eunuchs proved to be as ineffectual at government as they were at lovemaking. Their abuses eventually weakened the dynasty and left China open for invasion.

During Wanzu's reign, the most powerful eunuch was Kno Yang. This devious, high-pitched fellow was the head of the Ceremonial Bureau. As such, he supervised the Forbidden City and kept the emperor's date book. He wielded great authority, and court gossip held he, and not Wanzu, sat upon the Dragon Throne. The nobles hated him, and the generals wanted him dead. But Kno Yang only cared to win the hearts of the bureaucrats, believing that if he controlled the organs, the body would obey. Under his direction, the civil-service examinations—long a feature of Chinese society—took on even more importance.

It was in those days that two brothers with the surname of Kuan came up from the Shandong Province to take their exams in the capital. Tang, the older, was athletic, rugged, and given to drunken brawls. Han, on the other hand, was a serious student and aspired to be a landscape painter for the Imperial Court. Both were engaging, young men, though Tang was more likely to give or take offense.

They sat for their exams...and waited. When the test results were finally posted on the Imperial City's outer wall, they found that only one of them was accepted into service. To Han's relief, Tang showed no bitterness or disappointment. The brothers embraced, and both of them whooped with joy.

"You are a shengyuan!" Tang shouted, as he gave his brother a piggyback ride down the Outer City streets. "You will wear a cap and sash, and study with the masters!"

"Yes, yes, I am too important for you to speak to," teased Han, adopting a conceited tone. "Be silent and carry me to the Emperor, as fast as you can!"

Tang cared little for degrees and titles, but he knew his father took a different view. The thought of taking his failure home to his parents and ancestors was more than he could bear. Instead of heading for the family farm in Shandong, he wandered through the streets of Beijing. He took up with a violent gang and followed them to their camp in the remote, northwestern region of the Jingshi Province. There, in the shadow of the Great Wall, Tang participated in terrorizing travelers and extorting money from the locals.

Meanwhile, Han's painting career exploded like fireworks. The masters took note of his talent and good conduct. They advanced him along the chain of instruction leading to employment in the palace. In time, the ancient techniques became part of his nature. He perfected his brushstrokes, and his skill at mixing color was honed to precision. He far exceeded the other students at landscape painting, and his innovations were subtle enough to freshen the old traditions.

One day, Han was deemed worthy to attend a special banquet. Held in a lovely garden within the Forbidden City, it included several prominent members of the literati. They sat at a large, black-lacquered table and sampled culinary marvels such as aged duck and "Monkey Head." The music of a zither blended with the songs of the many caged birds that hung from the boughs of the fir trees.

When the meal was winding down with fresh apples and Dragonwell tea, a dialogue began between two of China's most respected philosophers. One of these was Old Chow, who had served the court faithfully for seventy years. He had a long, white beard, and a face that resembled a pug that had sucked on a persimmon. This elderly master was a favorite of the eunuchs because he was the watchdog of tradition. His lectures and writings on obedience had strengthened KnoYang's stranglehold over the country.

The other philosopher—and Chow's greatest rival—was Young Wang, whose moniker belied the fact that he was sixty-six years old. Young Wang believed that life could be improved, and he encouraged his students to break out of the old ways of thinking. He thought that China was too steeped in stagnant tradition. Needless to say, his opinions did not sit well with Old Chow.

"It is a sacrilege to honor your own ideas before those of the ancestors," Old Chow said, his hands tucked into his deep, silk sleeves. "It is conceit to sweep away the wisdom of the past."

"I do not hope to sweep away the past," answered Young Wang, "but to perceive it as it really was: flawed. If we question what we have been taught and test it with unflinching eyes, we may sift out unnecessary burdens from the lives of men."

"The ancient laws must never be changed!" Old Chow clenched his teeth, and his head shook with rage. "Confucian Canon is eternal! Would you rewrite the Five Classics and Four Books?"

"Perhaps not rewrite them, but I might reinterpret them."

"Ah, to serve your own needs."

"To serve justice and truth."

"There will be no justice if your philosophy prevails!" declared Old Chow. "There will only be chaos and insurrection."

"Let it come!" Young Wang bellowed. "Better to have chaos than tyranny."

"Tyranny?"

"Yes, tyranny, I tell you! Seventy-thousand eunuchs live in luxury at the palace and decide the fate of a 100-million people, and our emperor does nothing."

"You speak treason!"

"I speak the truth, and you know it," insisted Young Wang. "But why pick on the emperor and the eunuchs? Are we scholars any better? Do we not harness our pupils with tradition? Do we not say to our poets, 'Write only like this ancient poet', and to our painters, 'Paint only this established way?'"

"There is a right way and a wrong way to do anything, if one is seeking perfection," Old Chow said, stubbornly. "The Great Teachers are our only guides."

This debate might have gone on until dusk, had not a palace courier arrived with a message. He told them that the Imperial Court portrait painter was beheaded that morning and that the emperor demanded an immediate replacement. It was no secret to anyone that thirty-one Imperial Court portrait painters had lost their heads in the previous four months, so none of the assembled scholars jumped at the chance to fill the post. They hemmed and hawed, until their eyes fell upon Han.

"Didn't someone say you were a painter, Han Kuan?" asked Young Wang. "A talented painter?"

"I paint landscapes, Master," Han answered, shyly.

"Portraits, landscapes—what's the difference?" growled Old Chow. "Would it not be a sacred honor to paint your emperor, boy?"

"Wait," Young Wang said, seizing the opportunity to further chaff his rival. "This lad is correct in his thinking. He means to specialize. That's good. That reveals wisdom. We cannot sacrifice such a mind to the whims of imperial madness."

"You go too far, Young Wang!" Old Chow stood, and his disciples followed suit. "The emperor is divine! You will lose your head someday."

"It is too heavy, anyhow," retorted Young Wang, and his disciples laughed.

But old Chow saw nothing humorous in blasphemy. He found it particularly reprehensible in teachers. He pulled rank and ordered Han to accompany the courier.

Han was frightened as he was led past the yellow-roofed buildings, chanting monks, and armed guards. His legs shook when he entered the Imperial Throne Room and kow-towed before Emperor Wanzu, and his teeth chattered during Kno Yang's inspection of him. The chief eunuch disliked the young painter at once, and glared at him with outrage.

"Those fools sent us a boy!" Kno Yang squealed.

"Who cares how old he is, if he can paint?" Wanzu threw a pear at Han and asked, "Can you paint, boy?"

Han hesitated to answer. He did not want to deceive the emperor. He wanted to explain that he painted only sky, water, trees, and mountains; but he was tongue-tied. Kno Yang shuffled over in wooden, platform shoes, and slapped Han across the face.

"Answer your emperor!"

"Yes," said Han, rubbing his cheek and suppressing a desire to pummel the eunuch. "I can paint, Imperial Majesty."

"Well, then, you shall be my new Imperial Court portrait painter!" Wanzu let his hands fall into his lap, and looked about with childish glee. "I command you to begin my portrait now, Imperial Court Portrait Painter!"

"Have you tools?" Kno Yang asked Han. "Where are your paints?"

"I brought nothing," Han confessed.

Kno Yang swung his long queue in an arc, then huffily folded his arms. He called for paint, brushes, and silk, and several of his attendants scurried off to see to it. They returned with the articles in less than five minutes, and were scolded for their laggardness.

Han prepared himself for work. He set up the paints in the time-honored way and sat on his knees before them. He chanted, cleared his mind of negativity, and found his chi'i. Then he took a deep breath, opened his eyes, and studied the shapes and coloring of his subject's face. Before he could dip his brush, however, the emperor rose from the Dragon Throne.

"Stop, don't paint me like this!" he screamed at Han. "I want you to paint me in my new clothes." He signaled two eunuchs, who promptly disrobed him, exposing his naked body. "There, that's more like it."

"Oh, Imperial Majesty!" gushed Kno Yang. "Those are most beautiful clothes in all universe!"

The other eunuchs enthusiastically agreed, but Han knelt there, stunned and disgusted. He'd never seen a sight more repulsive. The emperor had the sagging breasts of an old woman, and his protruding bellybutton was the size of a duck's egg. Han could not bring himself to preserve such an image for posterity.

"Imperial Majesty," he said, boldly, "I will not paint a nude."

A gasp escaped the court, and murmuring commenced. Wanzu stumbled backwards into his throne, as though someone had pushed him. Kno Yang began hyperventilating and had to be helped to a foot-stool. Since no one interrupted him, Han continued.

"The fact is, Your Imperial Majesty, I do not paint portraits at all. I am a landscape artist."

"My robes!" demanded Wanzu, as he used his plump hands to cover his privates. When he was again clothed, he grabbed Han by the hair and addressed him, nose to nose. "You are fond of telling the truth, Han Kuan, but the truth is what I say it is. You understand?"

"Y-y-yes, Imperial M-m-majesty."

"Send him to the executioner!" shouted Kno Yang, for he was overwrought and losing it. "Slice head off shoulders!"

"Ah, I do not think so," Wanzu said, as he retook his Dragon

58

Throne. "I have already executed one Imperial Court portrait painter today. Moderation in all things. Besides, I have worse fate in mind for young Han Kuan."

"Ooo!" Kno Yang rubbed his palms together and slid across the floor on his knees to the emperor's feet. "Do tell."

"Well," began Wanzu, with a conspiratorial mug, "you know that the jinshi Xu You is a tedious man."

"And how! Xu You is forever quoting Confucian proverbs. Is worse than water torture."

"That's why I sent him to his castle in the Jingshi Province. The winds in that region are bitter, and the winter brings much snow. Xu You no like it. He prefer luxury of court."

"Too bad."

"Quite." Wanzu demurely covered his ankle with the hem of his robe. "But is not logical to make a dissatisfied governor. I think to please Xu You by sending him this boy. Han Kuan will paint pretty landscapes of tropical lands, and he will tutor Xu You's young daughter. The harsh, forlorn wilderness will give the painter more agony than a swift sword."

"Most clever, Imperial Majesty!" cried Kno Yang. "If the boy does not die of cold, he will choke on proverbs."

In this way, Han was exiled to the border reaches of the empire. He was taken far to the northwest, to the mountains that border Mongolia. The air was thin here, the temperature cold, and the wind whipped around the barren ridges. Though it was high summer, it felt more like late autumn to Han.

The jinshi, or educated official, Xu You lived in an ancient fortress perched on the edge of a cliff. It was enclosed by a series of watchtowers and a thick and ugly wall. Within the wall was a maze of equally dowdy, box-shaped buildings. Each had gray-tiled roofs with upturned eaves, from which hung chimes that tinkled or donged, depending on the strength of the gust. There were several courtyards: some with leafless trees, some with camelback bridges, and a few with shrines or fanciful pagodas. A grid of brick walkways veered at unexpected angles. The restless earth had buckled the bricks in places, and tree roots had done tremendous damage in their desperate search for minerals.

The central hall of this martial nest was externally unprepossessing. It was larger than the other buildings, but its façade held no additional distinction. Inside, however, was a mysterious world of treasures, clouds of incense, and secret passages. Gold, jade, jasper, porcelain, and silk—all were in abundance. They suggested past glory and hinted of bittersweet sagas.

Xu You received the artist gladly, for he was anxious to hear the latest court gossip. He ordered a banquet prepared; and while his servants dashed from building to building to meet this command, Xu You took Han on an extensive tour of the fortress. It was more of the same. The façades were bland and stoic; the interiors womblike.

Han paid his respects at the family ancestors' shrine. He met the elders and officers, two of Xu You's three wives, and all five of his concubines. The jinshi then led the way to his number-one wife and her daughter Ying-Ling.

Madame You was a gaunt woman, with the expression of a resolute martyr. The most she could give for a smile was a twitch of her thin, upper lip. She wielded her sadness against her husband, and she never abandoned her station. She was a devout Confucian, too, and she let Han know that he was expected to explore that discipline, exclusively, in the instruction of her daughter.

Ying-Ling inspired pity in all who looked upon her. She was nine-years old and fat as a dumpling. Her face was round and bloated; she had a pronounced overbite; and the orbits of her pupils were not synchronized. Han supposed her dim-witted, until she began a precocious homily on the dangers of the state of Zheng.

During the next few weeks, Confucian principles and the rituals of ancestor worship dominated Han's life. Every scroll he painted, every subject he discussed, and every move he made was subject to the mutated theologies of his master, his mistress, and even his student. Xu You followed Han about, spouting proverbs. Madame You dispensed guilt liberally, and her entrance into a room was like the passing of a cloud in front of the sun. As for Ying-Ling, she absorbed the piety of her parents and built upon it, to the point that her considerable intelligence was thwarted by caustic self-righteousness. By harvest time, Han had resigned himself to misery. And then...a miracle!

"We will soon have a special guest arriving," Xu You said to Han, one frosty morning, as they strolled through a courtyard. The jinshi's eyes gleamed with anticipation, and his stride was that of a young man's. "The most beautiful woman in all of China."

"Is so?" asked Han, snapping to attentiveness. "Is she a relative?"

"No, a courtesan. A famous courtesan. She is called 'Lady Plum,' for she is sweet, ripe fruit."

"I have never heard of her."

"Where is the wonder in that? She is not for men like you. I, myself, can barely afford her. You see, she is lovely beyond compare. She is also trained in conversation and skilled in the art of love."

"You are lucky man, Master," said Han, kicking a pebble. "Shall I meet her?"

"I expect so. You paint her for me, no? Then I shall always possess her in a small way."

Lady Plum's midnight arrival coincided with the Moon Festival. So when she alighted from her curtained sedan chair, she found the fortress bedecked with colorful lanterns and banners. Fireworks exploded, and Ying-Ling presented her with the traditional gift of moon cakes. Because the night was clear and cold, the party quickly moved into the central hall, where a firepot and a jug of kaoliang waited.

The courtesan was all that Han dreamed she would be and more. Her skin was creamy and luminous. Her eyes were kind, and though they were often lowered in submission, they flickered, now and then, with desire. Her figure was petite and exquisitely proportioned, and her feet were dainty. When she spoke, her voice was that of a songbird.

"I am most pleased to be in your lovely home," she said to Madame You, who nodded with the least civility expected. "It is my hope we will be friends and spend happy winter together."

"We not concerned with happiness here," Madame You answered, tersely. "We care only that we bring no shame to our ancestors."

"Lady Plum, are you going to kiss my father?" asked Ying-Ling, whereupon she was removed from the room.

The days passed into winter, and the snows marooned the fortress. The tea became watery, and the menu less varied. Just before the New Year, Xu You commanded Han to paint a portrait of Lady Plum. Though he had always prided himself on painting only landscapes, this was a portrait that Han embarked upon with zest. He packed his paints and rushed to the house in which the courtesan was staying.

"Why not paint two portraits?" Lady Plum asked him, as she lounged upon floor pillows. "One for your master and one for yourself. Would you like that?"

"I-I-I-I..." Han's mouth pulsed like that of a carp. "I-I-I-I..."

"It is pity you hesitate," she told him, "because you are too handsome for incompetence. Do you want a portrait of me, or not?"

"Oh, yes!"

"That is better." Lady Plum smiled, stood, and disrobed. "What is wrong? Do you not paint nudes?"

"Oh, yes!"

"Ah, I think you have never seen a naked lady," she teased. "You innocent? Don't be shy." She turned to her maid. "Go to the door and watch for spies, Yun-Li! I am going to teach this boy about pleasure."

From that moment on, Han could think of nothing but Lady Plum. He hung on her every word, and he found she had much to say. A Taoist, she believed in allowing things their natural course, and she recoiled from the control that Xu You and his family sought to exercise.

"Yield, do not assert," she quoted to Han, one day. "That is the law that governs my life. Why wrestle? Has wrestling put Madame You at peace? She try to manipulate, but she most hard on herself. She age fast. She not only rigid with her husband; she make his other wives and his concubines rigid, too. Everyone tense. Even you. I can't wait to get out of here."

It hurt Han to think that she was anxious to leave him. He was mad with desire and would have gladly taken his life for her, if she had bid him do so. She did not bid anything, but let everything come to her.

When the two paintings were completed, Han had no further occasion to visit Lady Plum. He kept the nude of her—rolled up on a bamboo scroll—under his bed. Each night, he took it out and pined.

Spring finally arrived, and the earth began to thaw. One bright, windy morning, Lady Plum climbed back into her sedan chair and waved a quick good-bye to Han and the others. They could hear her cheerful song long after she'd passed from their sight. Han wept.

A month or so later, he was dozing in his room when Ying-Ling opened the door and entered. Like the rest of the jinshi's household, the child had grown crabby and sullen since Lady Plum's departure. Han could tell the child had come with the express intention of annoying him.

"You should not be here, Ying-Ling," he told her. "This is my room."

"I know," she said. Each of her eyes independently searched the room for anything of interest. "I wanted to see where you are put when you're not wanted in the classroom."

Han sighed and closed his eyes. "Yield, do not assert," he thought, and he tried to release all his worry. He was vaguely aware that Ying-Ling was rifling through his things, but the master's child would do as she pleased, anyhow.

"This one of your scrolls?" she asked, unrolling the much-cherished portrait.

"Yes," answered Han, without opening his eyes. "All the scrolls in room are mine."

"This naked woman looks a lot like Lady Plum."

Han sprang from his bed and tried to snatch the scroll from Ying-Ling's hand, but the child went screaming, "Mama! Mama!" through the complex. He pursued and nearly caught her, but she found triumphant safety in her mother's arms. Madame You took one horrified look at the scroll and sent it to her husband. When Xu You saw it, he wept over Lady Plum's image and cursed her for her betrayal. He had Han thrown into the fortress dungeon and gave orders to behead him at dawn.

The dungeon had been hewn from the mountain, and it was cold and dank. A single torch burned beside an old, bronze gate. Han remained close by it, for the rest of the cave was pitch-black. The night hours dragged on, yet Han could not wish for morning. He drifted in and out of uneasy sleep until the calling of his name jolted him wide-awake. Fear lurched through him when he realized that the voice was coming from the dark of the cave.

"Han! Han!" Each shout echoed off the slate. "Han, come here! Come closer!"

"Who are you?"

"Your friend."

"Well, friend, step into light."

"Oh, lack of light bother you?" asked the voice. "I can remedy that."

Han heard and felt a huge intake of breath, and he had to hold

64

onto the gate to avoid being sucked into it. He nearly fainted when a blast of white flame exploded from the bowels of the cave. It illuminated everything so that Han could clearly make out the shackled skeletons, the flying bats, and the big dragon that was vomiting up the inferno. The flames licked at the dormant torches that lined the slimy walls. The torches flared to renewed life and continued to burn long after the dragon had ceased his pyrotechnical display.

"Han Kuan content, now?" The dragon smiled and scratched the side of his jaw with the joint of one of his wings. His scales were made of pure gold; his toenails were shards of jade; and his eyes shone like rubies held up to a candle. He was a glorious creature, and he knew it. His narcissism was evident in his smug tone when he said, "I am the Golden Dragon."

"Is pleasure to meet you, Golden Dragon."

"Yes, it would be, I suppose. I've come to bring you change, Han."

"That is kind of you, and timely."

The Golden Dragon giggled and snorted, and he expelled a blue flame from his backside. "Oops," he said, and snorted some more. "I hate when that happens."

"Am I going to die?" asked Han, fanning his hand in front of his face.

"Eventually."

"This morning?"

"No, not this morning." The Golden Dragon paused to bite off a hangnail, then he tenderly scooped the painter up in his wing. "Life now improve for you, Han. Not so many tribulations. But change lucky for some is unlucky for others, and change never walks earth without trodding grass."

"Huh?"

"You no listen to me!" The Golden Dragon was racked with spasms, and he coughed up some sparks and a few licks of flame. "What was I saying?"

"Trodden grass?"

"Ah, so! Here's the point: to every action, there is a reaction. Ah, must dash. Even Golden Dragon needs his beauty sleep."

He set Han onto the cave floor, wished him well, and pranced off down a dark passage. Han was left alone, but not for long. Hearing the jingle and clank of keys against bronze, he rushed back to the entrance of the dungeon and was amazed to find his brother Tang had opened the gate.

"Tang!" Han cried, hugging his brother. "How you come to be here?"

Tang explained how he and his gang ambushed and kidnapped Lady Plum as she returned to Beijing. He fell in love with the courtesan, and she fell in love with him. During an evening of sharing their pasts, she confessed maternal affection for a young painter named Han Kuan. Upon hearing that his little brother was exiled to a joyless fortress, Tang set off with his gang to collect him. He had every intention of being polite about the matter, but Xu You greeted the gang with disdain and rudeness. He called them "barbarians" and threatened to have them imprisoned with Han. So Tang, in a fit of rage, slew the haughty jinshi, whereupon Madame You flung herself off a watchtower and onto the jagged rocks. The child Ying-Ling was spared because she promptly handed over the keys to the dungeon.

"Come live at our camp," Tang suggested, when he had finished his account. "Or do you want to go back to Beijing?"

"A return to court is impossible," said Han. "The emperor would take my head."

"But don't you know?" asked Tang. He laughed and ruffled his brother's hair. "Wanzu die of smallpox."

"Is so?"

"Is so! And new emperor behead Kno Yang, right away."

Han gleefully received this news. After a month's visit with Tang and Lady Plum, he went to Beijing and resumed his career. He rose to the post of Imperial Court Landscape Painter. He married a sweet girl named Guan and a sour girl named Dou-Li. The new emperor presented him with a house in the Forbidden City and eight concubines. Best of all, Han got to keep his head...until the Manchu invasion.

Chapter 7

ANDRES AND ATAHULLPA

N A Peruvian hacienda thousands and thousands of feet up into the Andes, two rich men—both of whom claimed pure Castilian blood—sat in butternut-leather chairs before a fire. They smoked cigars, sipped their brandy, and held forth on political topics of the day. They were conservatives, monarchists, and loyalists, and any talk of Peru's independence rattled them considerably.

Don Augusto, the younger and larger of the two, owned the hacienda and the coffee plantation upon which it sat. Robust and big-mouthed, he usually got what he wanted. As a lad, he had traveled to Spain in search of a wife. He came home with Antonia, a beautiful aristocrat. When asked why she had chosen a colonial instead of a courtier, Dona Antonia answered that she had proved defenseless in the face of such a siege. Don Augusto was as head strong about business and politics as he was about wooing. Indeed, raw verve propelled every aspect of his life.

Don Velasco differed from his host in that he was a wiry, pockmarked hypochondriac. Incan slaves laboring deep in the earth provided him a fortune in gold and copper, but the master knew no peace. His wife had abandoned him; his two sons had killed each other in a duel; and his only surviving child Isabella could not conceal her displeasure at his company. His odious character won him few admirers. The governor did not respect him. The other mine owners plotted against him, and the Inca loathed him. He somehow withstood the onslaughts and spewed his bitterness back at the world. On this particular night however, he oozed charm.

"How I envy you, mi amigo!" he said, lifting his snifter to indicate the sweep of Don Augusto's comfort. "You have a handsome house, a pretty wife, and a fine son. To your credit, Andres is becoming a real gentleman. When does he return from Spain?"

"Soon," Don Augusto answered, his chest puffing with pride. "Andres has done well. He could go on to University, but what would be the point? He is a planter, not an intellectual. His place is here, in Peru—"

"With his papa!" added Don Velasco. "Will he choose a Spanish bride as you did?"

"There was talk of a certain senorita from Barcelona, but it came to nothing. I suppose he may choose a bride in Lima."

"But the girls in Lima are wicked, and most of them are tainted with Incan blood. Why don't you suggest that Andres look closer to home?"

"Closer to home than Lima?" Don Augusto asked, removing his boot to scratch at the toe of his stocking. "Oh, you are speaking of your daughter Isabella."

"Why not, amigo?" Don Velasco hugged the arm of his chair and leaned closer to his host. "Isabella may be difficult, but she will one day be very rich. I am certain Andres could tame her and, in doing so, combine our fortunes. They would be the richest couple in all South America. Think of it!"

"I am thinking," Don Augusto assured him. "I don't know why I haven't thought of it before, except that...well, Isabella has been a handful to you."

"Si, si," conceded Don Velasco, "but a woman needs aji in her. It will make life spicy for Andres. What do you say? Will you press for the marriage?"

"Uh..." Don Augusto's mind filled with the image of dancing bullion. "Si, I will point out the wisdom of such a union to Andres when he returns."

70

"To Isabella and Andres!" toasted Don Velasco. He winced as he took a gulp of brandy, then smacked his lips with satisfaction.

On the morning of Andres' arrival, the hacienda buzzed with activity. House slaves ran about, chattering in Quechua, and the cooks rushed to prepare mass quantities of papas and cuy, elsewhere known as potatoes and guinea pig. Don Augusto climbed a rickety ladder and hung the Spanish flag from an eave of the porchero, while Dona Antonia dispensed llama's milk to the mission boys' choir, who'd been hired to sing a Te Deum. It was all confusion when Andres arrived, but no one cared—such was their joy.

The party lasted all day and well into the night. Everyone—even the lowliest slave—ate too much, drank too much, and flirted too much. The music and dancing went on and on, but by dawn the court-yard was deserted. The flag whipped in the morning breeze, and flies gorged on rancid bowls of ceviche.

Andres, his head throbbing, cautiously climbed out of bed. He splashed water on his face and under his armpits and left his family sleeping. He slipped off to the grazing fields above the hacienda where, because the terrain was too steep and rocky to be terraced for coffee plants, sheep, alpacas, and llamas were raised for wool. It was a sunny day, and the animals were playful. Andres felt frisky too, as he climbed up to Ol' Mo's hut.

Ol' Mo was an Incan herdsman who lived with his granddaughter and a talking crow named Ha-Ha. Ever since he'd been a tot, Andres had been climbing up to eat boiled peanuts and purple corn and to glean wisdom from the herdsman. Ol' Mo knew things that others did not. He knew how to leave his body and fly around, and he could read minds.

There was another reason Andres was fond of climbing up that slope. Ol' Mo's granddaughter Quilla was two years younger than

Andres and about to become a woman. Her cheekbones were wide and high, her lips full and brown, and her eyes twinkled like brooches of jet. Her silken, black hair hung in braids to the small of her back. She was sensible, kind, and devoted to her grandfather, and Andres loved her with all his heart.

"You're home!" Quilla exclaimed, when Andres walked through the door. She then tempered her excitement by stepping back and adding a sarcastic, "And here I am without my ballgown!"

"Don't tease, Quilla," Andres told her. "Europe was a bore, and the women were vapid. I am glad to be home."

"And I am glad to hear it, Senor," she said, with a curtsy. "Come and see Grandpapa. He told me you were back from Spain, but I didn't dare believe it."

Ol' Mo sat with a colorfully woven blanket over his knees. His hands were relaxed with palms up, and his eyes were closed. A red, woolen cap was pulled over his sizeable ears, and a shock of white hair fanned out from beneath it. His face was wrinkled, his coloring gray, but a lively smile played upon his lips.

On his shoulder sat the crow Ha-Ha, who was getting on in years, himself. His feathers were sparse and dull, and a pocket of fat sloppily swung from his belly. His master had split his tongue and taught him to curse, and this education hadn't been wasted on Ha-Ha. When Andres approached, the crow turned sideways and squawked, "Buenos Dias, you stupid *#*#*#*!"

"Gracias, Senor Ha-Ha!" Andres replied, with a bow. "It is a pleasure to see you again, too."

Ol' Mo opened his eyes and laughed. He reached out and clasped Andres' hands. He fixed his eyes on him and would not look away—not even when tears streamed down his old cheeks. He said nothing for a long time. He just sat there, chuckling and squeezing Andres' hands. Finally, he let go, sat back, chuckled some more, and fed a boiled peanut to Ha-Ha.

In his own good time, he spoke. He asked many questions about

Europe. But before Andres could finish answering, Ol' Mo would nod, indicating he'd known the answers all along. He said he'd flown over Madrid often but had not bothered to drop in because he considered all cities to be glittering dung heaps.

"Si," agreed Andres. "I found them just as you say."

"Do you want to *#*#*#*?" asked Ha-Ha, strutting up and down his master's arm in a sort of waddle-march. "Show me your *#*#*#*!"

Ol' Mo laughed so hard at this profanity that he lost his breath. He gasped and held tightly to the arms of his chair. His face turned blue, and his eyes bulged. He stomped his feet and beat upon his chest. He clenched what teeth he had and grimaced. He got up and jogged around his chair three times before collapsing onto the beaten earth floor. There he writhed and thrashed. Then he crawled back to his chair, pulled himself into it, and fell asleep.

"Is your grandpapa okay?" Andres asked Quilla. He shooed away Ha-Ha, who'd gone frantically airborne. "Because he looks like he might be dead."

"No, he's fine," Quilla whispered. "He always has spasms when the spirit of Atahuallpa enters his body."

"The what of whom?"

"The spirit of Atahuallpa," said Quilla, nonchantlantly. "You know Atahauallpa? The great king of the Inca!"

"Si, I know who Atahuallpa was," Andres told her, "but what is he doing inside Ol'Mo?"

"He comes through once or twice a year, usually when he has something important to say. The last time, he came to tell us that one of our alpacas was impacted. Let's hear what he has to say today."

"I am the great Atahuallpa!" claimed the basso profundo spirit, speaking through Ol' Mo. "I am here to speak to Andres."

"Si," squeaked Andres, prompted by a nudge from Quilla. "Si, I am he. What do you want?"

"Listen to what I tell you!"

"Si, I am listening, Your Majesty."

"You must soon make a choice, Andres," Atahuallpa said, ominously. "A choice to please, or to be pleased. If you make the right choice, you will achieve both goals. If you make the wrong choice, you won't achieve either."

"This sounds complex, Your Majesty."

"It is, my boy! It is complex because life is seldom what it seems. Everyone wears a costume and mask, and who can tell who is who?"

"Do you know what he's talking about?" Andres asked Quilla. "I can't make sense of it."

"Shhh!" insisted Quilla.

"A man assumes many identities throughout his lifetime," Atahuallpa continued, "such as beloved child, struggling novice, and elderly statesman. Are you following me?"

"Uh... no."

"Well, never mind. You'll either work it out or you won't. Life is too often wasted on the living. Best of luck! We'll keep in touch from the other side."

Atahuallpa departed his host with none of the rigorous exercise that heralded his appearance. Ol' Mo opened his eyes and chuckled. He reached out to clasp Andres' hands again, then sat back and chuckled some more. He coaxed Ha-Ha back to his shoulder with a boiled peanut, closed his eyes, and went to sleep.

"Feel my *#*#*#*!" screeched Ha-Ha, hopping up to stand atop Ol' Mo's head. "Buenos Dias, you stupid *#*#*#*!"

When Andres returned to the hacienda that afternoon, a slave girl said his father wanted to see him in the library. He tapped at the door and entered to find his father going over the plantation books with the foreman. When the foreman was excused, Andres took his chair at the desk.

"How good it is to have you home, my son!" Don Augusto offered Andres a cigar then selected one for himself. "I expect you will find us boring after the marvels of Madrid, no?"

"No, Papa, not at all!"

"And yet, in all of Spain, you found no senorita to capture your heart?"

"Not in all of Spain, Papa."

"Ah, well," said Don Augusto, propping his big feet up on his desk. "Looks like your wife will be homespun."

"Si!" Andres enthusiastically agreed. "That is just what I have been thinking."

"Thinking is overrated, my son. I don't suppose you have a particular bride in mind—or do you?"

"Si, I do, Papa."

"Really?" Don Augusto took his feet off his desk and leaned forward, his cigar in a corner of his mouth. "Do you know, that's very funny, because I too have someone in mind. Can it be we are thinking of the same senorita?"

"Maybe," Andres said, doubtfully. "I don't know."

"Is it perhaps Don Velasco's daughter?"

"Isabella?" Andres crossed himself. "Heaven forbid!"

"Don't be hasty, son," Don Augusto cautioned. "Isabella may not be a beauty..."

"She's a cow!"

"She is a lady."

"You are right, of course, Papa."

"Andres, I speak to you as a man now. Passion—even the most ardent passion—is fleeting. Your mother is the most beautiful woman of her generation; even so, there are moments when we—when I cannot—when we content ourselves with kindness. Do you understand?"

"I think I hear someone calling me..."

"No one is calling you," Don Augusto said, irritably. "Sit back down! Andres, you will have children one day. Don't you want them to have every advantage?"

"Si, but what about love?"

"Ah, love!" Don Augusto threw his arms into the air, exasperated. "Love...love can be cultivated, Andres. Listen, if a man is handed a cup of coffee and it tastes good, he thinks, 'I am fond of this coffee.' But if a man plants a sickly bush, tends it with care, and nurses it until he has a thriving plantation, when he sips from his mug he will think, 'This is the best coffee in the world!'"

"Papa, a woman is not a mug of coffee," said Andres, weary of abstruse advice. "I will not marry Isabella."

"Then you are a fool!" Don Augusto shouted, rising from his chair to glower and puff. "Did they teach you this insolence in Spain, or did you learn it from that herdsman?"

"Leave Ol' Mo out of this, Papa."

"You went to see him this morning, didn't you? All these years, I've tried to keep you away from his corrupting influence... Still, you run to him the moment you are home. Why? The man is nothing but a slave, Andres. What could you possibly..." He broke off and sat down. "Or do you go to see the granddaughter? Is that it?"

"I love her," Andres confessed.

"Then take her for your mistress."

"No, I am going to marry her."

"No, you are not!" roared Don Augusto. "I will shoot you between the eyes before I let you marry an Incan slave!"

"Then do it."

"Don't be a child, Andres. You can't change the world. If you care for this girl as much as you say, you must stop toying with her. Such a marriage will never be tolerated in good Peruvian society. You are being cruel if you lead her to believe otherwise. They will hate her and any children she gives you, and you will grow to hate her too. You will break her heart, believe me. Is that what you want?"

"No," answered Andres, tears welling up in his eyes. "I never want to hurt her."

76

"Well, then!" Don Augusto came from behind the desk and put his arm around his son's shoulders. "These life lessons are sometimes hairy, but we must remember our Castilian blood. We must hold fast to our identity. Si, we should be just masters—of course! But we mustn't give the natives false expectations. You are a good man, Andres. I know you will do the right thing. Promise me you will not go up to that hut anymore. Promise me you will leave the herdsman and his granddaughter in peace."

"Si," Andres whispered, his tears now rolling down his cheeks and onto his shirt. "I promise."

Now no one considered Isabella a pretty girl...except Isabella. She had ratty, brown hair, plain features, and a noticeable mustache. Her torso was dumpy, and her arms were too long. Dark rings encircled her eyes, giving her the look of a masked bandit, and her chin was turned up and pointed. If she hadn't been born the daughter of Don Velasco, she would have probably burned at the stake. Nevertheless, she fancied herself a great beauty and spent hours before her looking glass.

The Velasco house slaves were scared of Isabella not only because they thought she looked like a demon but also because she behaved like one. She had fits of anger, howling and throwing things. She was more likely to beat a slave than not and was especially fond of pulling their hair, which she envied. Sometimes, whole weeks would pass without a civil word passing her lips, and many slaves ran off until her rage subsided.

But when Andres paid his first, formal call, signifying the beginning of a serious courtship, Isabella believed herself nigh on ecstasy. Here at last, she thought, was a man nearly her equal—a man to affirm her superiority and pledge his whole existence to her complete satisfaction. The slaves, bewildered to hear her singing, were suspicious of her kind words. They were right to be, for her euphoria did not last.

Upon Andres' second visit, Isabella detected flaws in him. He shuffled his feet, and his shoulders slumped. He breathed through his mouth, and a button was missing from his waistcoat. She admitted to herself that these imperfections were deceptively small, but she saw them as indications of a far worse problem—that of a lazy disposition. This was further evidenced in his manner of wooing. He showed no enthusiasm and seemed barely capable of conversation. As for compliments; why, she practically had to force them out of him, and afterwards he looked fatigued, as though leeches had sucked him bloodless.

Still, since it was unlikely that any rival suitor would claw up the Andes in search of her, she decided to settle on Andres. After all, she thought, such a mean little match was probably an unavoidable consequence of her colonial life. She had no intention of accepting him as found however, and set about trying to change him from top to bottom.

Andres was much annoyed at her attempts to transform him. He liked himself as he was, and he felt his own quiet tastes were preferable to Isabella's gaudiness. He was repulsed by her constant harping and her readiness to gossip about anyone, anywhere, anytime. In desperation, he complained to his father, who advised him to abide.

"Pretend to go along with everything she says," Don Augusto told him. "That is what men do when they are courting. After the wedding, you may do as you please."

"Papa, you don't understand," insisted Andres. "She is mad. She's obsessed with a matador she's never even met."

"What?"

"It's true! She once saw a newspaper sketch of him, and she began writing to him. He sent her back a lock of his hair, and she keeps it in a locket at her throat. She is trying to turn me into him. She makes me stand with my hand on my hip and my foot turned out, just so. Am I, a planter's son, to ape a vulgar matador?"

"It is her youth," said Don Augusto, shrugging his shoulders. "All senoritas are smitten with the matadors. It is the spectacle. The romance and suspense. In time, she will see the heroic qualities in you, and this silly infatuation will pass. Be patient and press on. I have no intention of releasing you from your promise."

So Andres continued his torturous visits to Isabella, but in his heart, Quilla remained his only love. He thought of her upon rising each morning. He thought of her when he washed, dressed, and ate. He thought of her at mass and dreamed of her at night. He especially thought of her when he visited Isabella.

"...and it will make all the women jealous," Isabella was saying, in her parlor one stifling afternoon. "Can you imagine what that bitch Senora Carraras will say when she hears of it? Sit up, Andres, and pull your shoulders back! And even your mother will wish she'd thought of it first. Close your mouth and breathe through your nose! This will be to your betterment, as well. That is why I want you to go to La Paz."

"What?" asked Andres, who'd been lost in a reverie of Quilla. "La Paz? Why should I want to go to Upper Peru?"

"To get Senor Alvarez and bring him here."

"Who is Senor Alvarez?"

"The matador!" cried Isabella, with impatience. "Do you never listen to a word I say? I wrote to Senor Alvarez, asking him to come fight in Papa's little bullring, and he has agreed!"

"It will cost Don Velasco dear, I imagine."

"Oh, what is money when one might bask in the company of a great artist like Senor Alvarez?" Isabella flipped open her black-lace fan and pumped hot air across her face. "You do not understand anything about culture."

At first, Andres resented Isabella's request, for he found such an errand beneath him. But the more he thought on the idea, the more he liked it. A journey to Upper Peru—known today as Bolivia—would mean hiking along the ancient Incan messenger trails and crossing Lake Titicaca. It would take at least a month and probably two. Two blessed months away from Isabella and her nagging. He sat up, straightened his shoulders, and said, "When do I leave?"

He took a couple of his best Incan scouts and a mule and set off southward. The steep trails were treacherous, and the mountain fog was often so thick that Andres could not see where he was placing his feet. One of the scouts and the mule were lost into a chasm. The remaining scout, distraught over his buddy's death, blubbered for seven days. He surely would have blubbered an eighth, had he not fallen off the ferry and drowned in Lake Titicaca.

When he arrived, Andres was pleasantly surprised at the vitality of La Paz. It was not as fashionable as Lima, to be sure, but it was clean and bustling. The mid-day sun saturated everything, from the orange-tiled roofs atop the brightly painted houses to the snow-covered peak of Illimani, sparkling in the distance. Black smoke puffed from the chimneys, censing the streets with burning llama manure. Cholo women bore baskets of papas on their heads, and Jesuits rushed to the noon Angelus. Andres was charmed.

He wasn't charmed by Senor Alvarez. The matador was cocky, rude, and prone to sulking. He was a dandy who dressed in short jackets, extremely tight trousers, and ruffles at his wrist. He wore heavy scent, and his greased, black hair gleamed like the surface of a pond. From the time he left La Paz until the time Andres deposited him safely at Don Valesco's hacienda, Senor Alvarez hardly ceased complaining.

"I dare not take another step," he often said to Andres during the course of their journey. "Is this danger really necessary? Can't we go around the mountains? Ai, ai, ai!"

Isabella—so quick to critique Andres—recognized no deficiencies in her matador. In fact, she fell instantly in love with him. He spoke to her in French and kissed her hand; she blushed, giggled, and fluttered her eyelashes. He lavished her with compliments and kissed her wrists; she tapped him on the head with her fan and called him a naughty nino. While kissing Isabella's gold adorned neck, the matador appraised the hacienda, the luxurious furnishings, and the pretty slavegirls. Isabella swooned in his arms.

This behavior did not go unnoticed by Don Velasco, and he was alarmed by this wolf's pursuit of his lamb. His stomach sickened at the sight of his daughter throwing herself at the feet of someone he could only describe as a shameless gigolo. He finally went to Andres and begged him to ask for Isabella's hand in marriage. Caught off guard, Andres requested the afternoon to think about it. He bowed to Don Velasco and walked off alone down a path which led to the mines. He'd only descended a few feet when he came upon Senor Alvarez. The matador was basking in the sun, gnawing on a branch of a coca shrub.

"Tell me," said Andres, "are you ever going to fight a bull? You have been here three weeks already."

"What, are you implying something?" Senor Alvarez speedily asked. He spit out some leaves and lifted his chin defiantly. "Why should I fight a bull when I have Don Velasco, eh?" He stood and paced. "How is it that Don Velasco should prefer you for a son-in-law? I am a far more worthy man! I am a world-class matador—an idol to women! You are a bumpkin who has only been to Europe once in your life. I am the better match for Isabella. You see, I know how to make women happy."

"You are a fortune hunter, a cad, and a sloth," Andres told him honestly, "and Don Velasco is not blind. He will never trust you with his daughter or his mines."

"He is a heartless man and so are you!" Senor Alvarez petulantly pulled another leaf from the coca shrub and bit off half of it. "How can that old man dare deny his daughter passion? Am I not a gift from heaven for that ugly shrew? I ask you, what is the use of being a famous lover if one cannot get past the papa? I might as well be some bumbling oaf. I might as well be you!"

In those days, most gentlemen faced with such an insult sought satisfaction, but Andres took no offense. He had no respect for the matador and was therefore unmoved by his opinions. Even so, the fellow's last six words struck a chord within Andres. He suddenly remembered Atahullpa's question: "Who can tell who is who?"

"That's it!" he shouted.

"What?" asked Senor Alvarez, startled.

"You might as well be me! And so you shall!" Andres grabbed the matador and began tugging on his jacket. "Take off your clothes!"

"Ai! Senor!"

"Do as I say, Stupido! We've no time to lose!"

Don Velasco was fond of his siesta and demanded absolute quiet while he took it. Unfortunately, his bedroom faced the West and the rays of the sun beat against it from afternoon until sunset. He had often cursed the poor architectural planning of his ancestors, and he did so again the same afternoon that Andres had gone off to contemplate matrimony. The sunlight seeped through cracks in the bedroom shutters and cast a sliver of light across Don Velasco's eyes. He rolled to the other side of the bed, but within minutes, the light again found his eyes. He put his arm across his face and fretted over the future of his money, daughter, and health. Suddenly, a racket started up in the courtyard.

"Don Velasco!"

"Hm?" Don Velasco sat up in bed. "What?"

"Don Velasco!"

It was the matador's voice. Don Velasco was enraged to think that the impudent rake would disturb his siesta. He got out of bed, hobbled across the room, and threw open the shutters. Light blinded and encompassed him, and he had to feel his way out onto the balcony. He squinted down at the courtyard and distinguished a crowd. All his house slaves were gathered before him, and his daughter and two men stood with their backs to the sun. He could not make out the faces of the two men, but one of them was bedecked in the garb of a matador.

"Papa!" Isabella shouted up to him, shrilly. "We thought you would never awaken!"

"What is it? What's the matter?" Don Velasco shouted back to her. He shaded his eyes with the crook of his arm. "Has a mine collapsed? Is there rebellion? Why is Alvarez standing there doing nothing? Who is that fellow in black? Is it Andres? What do you all want?"

"Papa!" Isabella gathered up her skirts and moved closer to the balcony. "I have a question for you."

"Ah, what bullshit is this?" growled Don Velasco, and he picked up a terra cotta pot and threw it down to shatter on the cobblestones. "You woke me up for a question? You know my siesta is sacred!"

"But it is the most important question of my life!"

"Si, Isabella, there is a God!"

"No, Papa," Isabella said, kicking aside shards of terra cotta to step closer still. "It is the question of my marriage."

"Marriage?" cried Don Velasco. "Has Andres proposed to you?"

"Si, Papa, and so has Senor Alvarez."

"What?" Don Valesco hurled a pot at the man in the matador suit, missing him by inches. "No ridiculous bullfighter is going to marry the daughter of Don Velasco!"

"Papa, stop throwing things! You'll kill someone!" Isabella shook her finger at him. "Behave! I am only doing this because I want to please you. I want you to decide for me. Tell me which of these two men I should marry, and the slaves will bear witness against me, should I ever go against your final decision."

"Very well," agreed Don Velasco, "I choose—"

"No, wait a moment, Papa!"

Isabella took the fellow in the matador suit and placed him to the left. Then she placed the fellow in black to her right. She resumed her spot and stretched out her long arms in supplication to the balcony.

83

"Shall I marry the man to my left, or should I marry the man to my right?"

"Aren't you ashamed to ask such a question?" Don Velasco rebuked her. "I will never allow you to marry that fiend in carnival clothes!"

"Then you want me to marry this man to my right?"

"Have you been out in the sun, Isabella? Si,si, the man to your right, the man in black, the man we know as—"

"And you will never go back on your word, Papa?"

"What?" He clutched his chest. "Don Velasco, go back on his word? Never!"

"Gracias, Papa!" exclaimed Isabella, and she blew her father a kiss. "I see now that you are more wise than you know. Please return to your siesta."

Don Velasco shook his head, stepped back into his bedroom, and closed the shutters. 'There,' he thought, 'that matter is solved.' He curled up in bed and promptly fell asleep. It was the last good sleep he would know in his lifetime.

As soon as Andres wished the newly betrothed all his best, he climbed out of the matador garb and back into his own clothes. He ran home and told his father that Don Velasco had settled on Senor Alvarez for a son-in-law. Don Augusto was livid.

"This is a slap in the face—an issue of honor!" he told his son, as he removed his dueling pistol from a drawer of his desk. "How dare that mine owner refuse MY son!"

"No, Papa, put that away and let things be," said Andres, with new strength to his voice. "This is the will of Heaven. Let Isabella marry whom she will. I accepted your choice of bride; now you must be a man and accept mine."

"You don't mean..." Don Augusto was appalled. "You can't mean that squat, little Incan girl!"

"Her name is Quilla, Papa, and there is nothing less than lovely about her. She is my heart's desire, and I am going to marry her. You'd better get used to the idea."

"I see you are determined," said Don Augusto, collapsing into his chair. "Well, you had better have my blessing. You will need it."

Andres found Quilla gathering her sheep in the high pasture. She saw him coming in the twilight, so she tossed off her ribboned hat and let her crook fall to the ground. He ran to her, embraced her, and spun her around and around. Then he passionately kissed her and wiped away her tears.

"We are going to be married!" he shouted, gleefully.

"Si, I know," she answered.

"How could you know? I only found out myself this afternoon."

She giggled, put her mouth to his ear and whispered, "Atahullpa told me."

Chapter 8

HORTENSE AND THE LEPRECHAUN

SEACROSS WAS ONE OF THE OLDEST HOUSES IN DEVONSHIRE, but was rarely acknowledged as such. It had only eleven rooms— scarcely a manor at all—and the guidebook editors considered it too diminutive to warrant the attention of their presumably well-heeled readers. Humble, it may have been—with its half-timbered walls, thatched roof, and crooked chimneys—but taken for what is was, it charmed the eye.

The master of Seacross was Sir Edward Peters, a gentleman from an unremarkable family who had made his fortune in trade. He cared little for society, which made him a favorite of society. To please his lovely wife Barbara, his two sons, and his six daughters, he also kept a house in Bath, another at Southhampton, and one in Grosvenor Street, London. These additional residences were fashionable, but Sir Edward preferred the comfort of his boyhood home. Whenever there was a lull in the heady whirl of commerce and social seasons, he whisked his family south to Devonshire for the good sea air and the absence of artifice.

Although most of the children complained, Barbara indulged her husband in these regular visits. She felt no harm in them, provided the weather was fine. Edward had begrudged her nothing in their years together, so she thought that giving him a bit of pleasure was the least she could do.

As time passed however, these journeys became less and less convenient. Things changed. Two of their daughters died of consumption, and the eldest married a viscount. The sons, always competitive brats, grew up to be no less so. Tom, the older, signed on with Wellington's men, determined to achieve glory on the battlefield. His brother Bertie went to sea with the fleet. The remaining daughters were ripe for picking, and London was abundant with gentlemen and officers. To Barbara, it seemed pointless to drop everything and travel a very uncomfortable distance, merely to sit at her needlework.

Nevertheless, she was unwilling to prohibit Sir Edward's joy, and she thought she'd come upon a solution. She broached it at breakfast one Saturday, when two of the girls were off to a country house party, leaving her alone with Sir Edward and their middle-daughter Hortense. She waited until her husband finished his kippers, then she plunged.

"Edward, we must have a word."

"Only one?" he asked, feigning grievance by clutching his napkin to his chest. "Do not be miserly, my dear. Be generous and spend more than one word upon the subject—whatever that subject may be."

"The subject is Seacross and whether or not the girls and I ought to join you."

"Whether or not?" repeated Sir Edward. "Whether or not? What the deuce does that mean? Speak plainly, Barbara."

"I must question the logic in quitting London when there is yet worthy activity," she replied. "His Majesty has remained late in town, and Lord Haverfield's ball is Saturday-next. Margaret and Nancy should stay and be seen."

"And what of Hortense?" Sir Edward asked, with a nod to his favorite daughter. "Is she not to be seen, hm? Shall we chain her in the scullery?"

"Hortense cares naught for dancing; she's like you in that respect. I do not say that anything is wrong with her appearance. She has some fine features. It is her morose nature that vexes me—and the men too, make no mistake. She cares only for reading, and pondering, and what-all. I'm sure I don't know what I may have done to encourage her lack of gaiety."

"You speak of our Hortense as though she were not here," said

Sir Edward, with a wink in his daughter's direction.

"She isn't here," was Barbara's reply. "She isn't ever HERE. Our opinions, mirth, or death can never hope to distract the girl from her musings."

"You are peevish this morning, my dear." Sir Edward smiled, sympathetically. "It must be the pudding served at Mrs. Findley's. I know it kept me tossing through the night. Let us postpone this discussion 'til our discomfort ebbs."

"Understand, Hortense," his wife continued, turning to her daughter. "I do believe you to be...an intelligent girl...with some fine features, but you possess that sort of coloring that is not enhanced in-of-doors."

"Really, Barbara!"

"I speak nothing but the truth, Edward. Her complexion and her temper darken in London. She becomes...gray. Oh, she does nicely in the country, where formality is a sign of ill-breeding; but stick her in a ballroom, and people take her for a governess. You do know, Edward, that she was invited to Kent with her sisters? She declined."

"They desired not my company, ma'am," Hortense said, matter of factly. "The Lindley's cannot see the consequence of me."

"Indeed, neither can I, if you will see no consequence in others." Despite the morning hour, Barbara poured herself a port from the decanter on the sideboard. "But if you feel yourself superior..."

"You are being unjust, dear," cautioned Sir Edward. "I have seen overwhelming evidence of Hortense's compassion. I will go further and say that I know of no member of this family that can equal her attentiveness to others."

"She is not attentive to the RIGHT others."

"You are correct," Hortense admitted to her mother. "I am hopeless in fashionable company, and I stand unrepentant in my affection for the countryside."

"Just as I said!" Barbara belted back the remaining port in her glass and turned to pour herself another. "That is why I suggest that you accompany your father to Seacross, whilst I remain in London with your sisters. Is that agreeable to you, my lamb?"

"Well, Hortense?" Sir Edward asked. "What do you say to this proposition, eh? Are you predisposed to help your old papa to Devonshire?"

"I would be delighted, Father."

"I am glad to hear it, child." Sir Edward rose to go to his mercantile offices. "I've no doubt that in Devonshire we shall meet with company more akin to our morose natures."

Sir Edward and Hortense left within the week. It was the first time they'd been alone on such a journey, and they sparred a little in the carriage. Hortense labored to introduce topics to engage and impress her father, but he remained detached and thoroughly unimpressed. When she sought to offer her opinion on the subject of Roman Catholic emancipation, Sir Edward scoffed and said she was insufficiently informed to speak of politics. Mortified, she fell silent and pretended to absorb herself in the passing terrain. As they neared the Devonshire coast however, conversation resumed between them; and by the time they reached Seacross, their exchanges became lively.

How happy the father and daughter were in Devonshire—happy to do as they pleased, to read and eat what they wished, and to go where and when they chose. In London, they habitually surrendered to the blunt-force will of those they held dearest. Now, at Seacross, they surrendered only to nature—to the salty breezes and the haze-diffused sun. It was bliss while it lasted.

On the sixth morning of their stay, Hortense was combing the shore for shells and oddities when she came upon a trio of French naval scouts. She screamed for help, but the roar of the waves smothered her pleas. She tried to flee, but the sand was deep and the rocks were slippery. The scouts gained on her and halted her escape.

They were common men but not without Gallic gallantry. They doffed their hats and introduced themselves in broken English. The one called Junot was apparently the leader of their reconnaissance mission. He was a high-strung Parisian, several inches shorter than Hortense, and he strutted like a rooster when he crowed his commands. His Gascon companions, Jean-Jacque and Jean-Luc, could have passed for identical twins. Both were tall, swarthy and slack-jawed, and both were missing an eyetooth. They profusely apologized to Hortense as they bound her with rope and led her down the beach. They helped her into a dingy, climbed in themselves, and rowed out to sea.

"Mon Dieu!" exclaimed Junot, as he sat opposite Hortense's scowl. "Do not distress yourself so, Mademoiselle. We mean you no harm."

"I'm not afraid of you, frog!"

"Pfft!" Francois shrugged. "I would rather dine well on delicacies than stuff myself with steak and kidney pie. Besides that, Mademoiselle, when Bonaparte liberates England, you will become une femme Française, non?"

"Jamais!" Hortense declared, defiantly.

As she watched Seacross fade from view, tears of despair rolled down her cheeks. She looked for means of escape, but the ropes defeated her. She was helplessly borne into a bank of fog and taken captive aboard a French frigate bound for Boulogne. The crew leered at her, but their captain—a sausage-nosed, weatherworn Britton named Delacoeur—treated her with civility. He silenced his men's catcalls and relinquished his cabin to serve as her cell.

True, Hortense was now a prisoner, but she never feasted as well as she did that night. Rich and varied dishes were brought to her, including Potage a' la Fantasque and Joint of mutton a' la Daube. Her Anglo-prudence necessitated a token cluck of her tongue, but she could not help but savor the tasty creations. The wine—the captain's best—

she found equally appealing, and she actually moaned over the dessert, an elaborate pastry that would have been considered scandalous aboard an English vessel. She climbed into the captain's bed, stuffed to capacity and slightly drunk.

She awoke in the pre-dawn hour when the frigate pitched dramatically. She soon learned they had run into a gale, the intensity of which surpassed anything Captain Delacoeur had ever seen. He ceaselessly fought throughout the morning and into the afternoon, barking orders and laboring beside the sailors. By nightfall, it was clear his efforts were futile. The ship had been blown far off course to the northwest, and she was listing. She was heavy with water and sinking.

For the next hour, Hortense moved as if in a dream. She became so violently ill that she had to be helped into a dingy. When the dingy was launched, a gigantic wave crashed over it and swept away the Frenchmen who were to pilot. Another wave followed close behind, and Hortense was sent flying into the cold ocean. She bobbed, disoriented and incredulous, as the frigate capsized and sunk. A piece of flotsam banged her head, and she was sucked down and down by the churning water. Memories of Seacross and her father flashed through her mind before she slipped into unconsciousness.

When she came to, she found herself washed onto a beach. Her body was sore and bruised, and she coughed up copious amounts of saltwater. The noonday sun beat down on her, and ocean spray stung her back. She crawled across the sand and pebbles and climbed onto a rock. As she wrung the water from her hair and shredded dress, she studied the topography.

It was a narrow, rocky strip of beach, and high cliffs hugged the shore. Hortense could just make out sloping pastures that lay far above her. They were not dissimilar to the pastures at Seacross, except for their astounding colors. Shades of green—some more vibrant than the first shoots of March—glimmered in the sunshine, then deepened under a passing cloud. In spite of her predicament, Hortense was enchanted. She summoned her energy and courage and climbed to the top of the cliffs.

When she had pulled herself to safety, she found a sea of grass stretching as far as the eye could see. Not a cottage, not a road, not even a tree was in sight. She despaired, thinking herself doomed to starvation. Racked with sobs, she fell to her knees and pounded her fists in the earth. When she was quite done, she staggered to her feet, tidied her hair, and began to trek inland.

She was elated when she spotted a rock wall, then another, and another, and another. She was astounded to come upon a stone cross of unmistakably Celtic design. She rightly supposed herself to be in Ireland, and she chuckled at the absurdity of her situation. A chilling, steady rain began to fall, and thunder shook the ground beneath her; still, Hortense persevered. It was dusk when she reached a cottage, and she was almost past caring by then.

It was an odd cottage, built half under a hill. It was white washed and green-shuttered, and candlelight gleamed from its windows. The roof was turf, and turf smoke rose from the chimney. It seemed a welcoming home, so Hortense took a deep breath and stumbled up the walk. But as she reached for the big, brass knocker, a peculiar fellow threw open the door to greet her.

He was no taller than a child of six, though his feet were as wide as a man's. He wore a wee, green suit with gold buttons, and gold buckles adorned his shoes. His hair was as orange as a harvest pumpkin, and his round face was flecked with tawny freckles. Mischief twinkled in his Irish eyes, and he grinned from pointed ear to pointed ear.

His size belied his strength. When he pulled Hortense inside, she went tumbling like a rag doll. He propped her up in a chair by the fire and put a rug over her legs. He spoon-fed her potato soup and moistened soda bread. He poured thimble-fulls of whiskey down her, and threw a couple back himself. She began to revive; he pulled up a stool and fired up his pipe.

"Sure now, this is a nice surprise!" he said, in a high, lilting voice. "You've been shipwrecked; that's common enough in this part of Cork."

"Is that so, sir?" asked Hortense, a tad testily, for it annoyed her to hear her plight—her ordeal!—casually dismissed as common. "I thought you said it was a nice surprise."

"You're quick to take offense, for someone in need of a friend," he told her, then blew a smoke ring that spun through the air to wreath the top of her head. "You're all alone, save me. And nary a soul survived with you, I'll wager, for it was banshee weather we were having last night. I've seen it happen time and again on this coast. It's as common as green. You're lucky to be alive."

"I am contrite, sir. Pray, forgive me."

"Nay, lass," he said, flustered. "There's no apology needed." He stuck out his hand. "The name's Rory O'Darby. I'm a leprechaun!" He jumped on his stool, put his hands on his hips, and began to merrily jig. "You know, lass: pots of gold, impish shenanigans, and a few good magic tricks!"

"I must be delirious," Hortense said to herself. She shook her head a couple of times, then pressed her palms to her temples. "I'm sorry to say, Mister O'Darby, that I do not follow you. It has been quite a day, you understand?"

"I do, I do," Rory assured her. "Come along, and I'll show you to your room. You can have a nice, long sleep."

Rory led her to a paneled bedroom with a sprightly turf fire and adequate toiletries. He left her a fat beeswax candle, bid her say her prayers, and blew her a friendly kiss good night. Shutting her door, he danced on down the hall.

Weary as she was, Hortense still managed to kneel on her bruised knees and give thanksgiving for her deliverance. She then climbed snugly into a sleigh bed, which had a down-filled mattress and a half-dozen colorful quilts. She felt safe, content, and even a trifle giddy. She listened to Rory sing a lullaby as he washed up the pots and pans. Sweet sleep took her suddenly and deeply. She did not wake for another nine hours.

A new day dawned, the cock crowed, and the birds began to warble. The rain stopped, and Hortense instinctively knew that—whatever the problems of the past—things were now taking a turn for the better. She rose from the cocoon of her bed, washed herself, and disciplined her curly, brown hair. After making her bed, she went in search of Rory.

She found him cooking sausages over the hearth. He sat her down to a hearty breakfast and a mug of foaming ale. While she ate, he gave her a tune of his own composition. He played it first on the fife, next on the fiddle, and then sang it, a cappella. His tears fell like rain, and his voice broke, when he got to the part where Brian Boru was struck down at the Battle of Clontarf.

Hortense listened and ate until she could eat no more. Rory climbed up beside her on the bench. He again told her that he was a leprechaun and added that he'd been around for five hundred and thirteen years. Even after getting a good look at him in the daylight, Hortense remained unconvinced. To prove it to her, Rory vanished from sight. He returned a moment later to find her face gone ashen, so he poured her another ale.

He took her outside and pointed to a rainbow that straddled the kelly-green pastures. He grabbed her by the hand and took off running so that she had no choice but to follow. They ran and ran until they reached one leg of the rainbow, and they danced about in the glittering prism. Somewhere between the green and orange bands sat a pot of gold, stuffed to overflowing. Rory climbed in to bathe in the coins, biting a couple to illustrate their authenticity.

"What do you think of the ol' leprechaun now?" he asked. He giggled, squealed "Wee!", and wallowed in the gold. "It's all yours, lass, every bit of it. I've got plenty, meself, stashed away in a secret hole beneath a magical tree."

"I am astonished, sir!" exclaimed Hortense. "It is miraculous. I will be able to purchase my passage to England."

"England?" Rory lost his grin. He climbed out of the pot, kicked it, and made it disappear. "Why England? I thought you were happy here. Far be it for me to increase the number of English boars in this country, but you're not a boar at all. You have some fine features. I want you to stay."

"I am happy," she assured him. "You've been most kind. But my family will be concerned, and I must return home. I am bound to think of my future and secure a husband."

"Make your future in Ireland," Rory insisted. "If your family wants you, they'll find you. 'Tis said a life not lived in Ireland is no life at all. Why, there's been no magic in England since Merlin. And if it be a husband you're after, there's none can top the men of Cork at lovin'. As a matter of fact, I know just the man for you. His name is Samuel Butterfield, and he's a decent-looking feller. Ah, sure now, you'll take a shine to him, lass."

"Is Butterfield an Irish name?"

"He's Anglo-Irish, but I don't hold his birth against him. He's got five thousand pounds a year coming in, and that will buy a lot of pretty dresses. He has a manor and stables, and his tenants never bicker or rise. What do you say, lass? Take a peek at him?"

"I must be cautious, Mister O'Darby," Hortense answered, the blood rising in her cheeks. "You say that Mister Butterfield is handsome..."

"I said he was decent-looking."

"You said he was decent-looking, comfortably well-off, and blessed with good tenants, yet you did not disclose his age. Are you able to find me a young man?"

"I'm a leprechaun, lass, not Saint Patrick. But Samuel Butterfield cannot be that old. I would put him at forty."

"Forty!"

"Well, what is the point of marrying a rich man if he's going to outlive you?" Rory asked. "Besides, he's youthful in appearance, and his nature is very childlike."

"I suppose it would do no harm to look at the man," Hortense said, weakening. "If, as you say, he's five thousand a year."

"There, now! That's the Irish way to look at things!" Rory told her, and he pulled a flask from his jacket and took a nip or two. "Did I happen to mention that Samuel lost a leg in Spain? Ah, here lass! Have some of this poteen. It's magically delicious!"

So Hortense agreed to be introduced to Samuel Butterfield before she sailed for England. Rory arranged everything, though he refused to accompany Hortense onto "occupied" soil. She set out alone for Butterfield's manor, called Round House because of its Palladian design. She found it a huge, rambling residence showing numerous signs of neglect. Upon entering, she noticed that the plaster was cracked, that there was a thick layer of dust on the tables, and that the curtains were unraveling. Packs of hounds roamed throughout the rooms, and more than one servant dozed in quiet corners.

As for Samuel, he was no tidier than his house. His hair was long and disheveled, his coat was spattered with mud from his morning ride, and his cuffs were yellowed and frayed. Although it was true he had only one leg, it was a fine one. Its muscles bulged beneath the tight riding boot and the stretch of his almond-colored britch.

He was woefully absentminded, often forgetting he had a guest. But each time he happened to notice Hortense, it was obvious he was smitten. He called for tea and cakes, and they arrived within the hour. He requested that Hortense pour and took delight in watching her do so.

"Tell me, Miss Peters," he said, "where is your home?"

"In Devonshire, sir, as I have said," answered Hortense, some-what frustrated. "But my father has houses in Southhampton, Bath, and London. You mentioned earlier that you disdain London. I daresay you've every reason to find it disagreeable, but do you frequent Dublin?"

"Where?"

"Dublin," she repeated. "Dublin, Ireland?"

"Ah, yes," replied Samuel, with vague recognition. "Yes, there are a lot of folk there."

"I should say, sir."

"I don't care for a crush," he told her. "I prefer dogs, horses, and the beauty of County Cork. You may as well know, Miss...uh..."

"Peters," Hortense reminded him.

"You may as well know, Miss Peters, that I'm a complete fool at balls and parties. I can't put a foot right—never could, not even when I had two."

"I understand, Mister Butterfield. I'm something of the same. I often wish for a quiet, country life and would not be sorry were I never again to mix in fashionable company."

"You would quit society?"

"That depends on the emphasis given the word, sir. If by 'society' you refer to those who give themselves over to dictates, gossip, and insincerity, then yes, I would not grieve to part from it. But if by that same term you mean those who choose their friends for their character, who desire not the cachet of a connection but the honest friendship it may bear, then I should not want to quit it, entire."

"Well put, well put," Samuel said, his bovine eyes blinking with admiration. "It would seem we have much in common, Miss Peters. Tell me, where is your home?"

As Rory had thought, Samuel Butterfield was the man for Hortense. She married him as soon as their bands were read in the village Anglican Church. They then sailed to England and Seacross. Not a single member of Hortense's family approved of her scatterbrained groom, but she didn't care a fig. She was happy in love with a one-legged Irishman, and she thought him magically delicious.

The couple returned to Round House, had fourteen children, and were jolly more days than not. Samuel went to his grave first—hit by a train at age ninety-six. Hortense was left a rich widow, but she never smiled again. Not fully two months after her husband's death, she was laid to rest beside him in the Butterfield family crypt. As for Rory, he lives on in Cork still, chasing rainbows and distributing gold.

Chapter 9

SUSIE-JO AND THE GENIE

USIE-JO WAS A FINE-LOOKING GAL—BUXOM, WITH GOLDEN curls and a pert nose—but it was her misfortune to live in an age of desolation. Had she been born at an earlier time, she would have been one of the richest, prettiest belles in a rich and pretty society. Instead, at seventeen, she found herself in rags, subsisting on beans, collard greens, and rice. Her beloved mama had been carried off by yellow fever, her brother Joe-Joe blown to bits at Manassas. Her family's plantation, along with most of South Carolina, had been pillaged and burnt to a crisp. All she now had left in the world was her father Charlie, a broken ghost of a man. A broken ghost she treasured beyond measure.

"Lord, how the mighty are fallen!" she would quote to herself, as she weeded the pitiful vegetable patch that sat next to the ruins of the big house. "Pride goeth before a fall!"

She knew her Scripture fairly well, on account of Charlie. He was a pious man, steeped in ol'-timey tenets from which he never budged. Amidst the ruins, he called out to his wrathful angels and shook his praying hands at stormy Heaven. To him, Armageddon was a sweet name, and he eagerly awaited the Four Horseman of the Apocalypse.

Since the war, Charlie rarely left the fishing shed. The old cypress-wood structure had been spared the torch because it sat in the middle of a gator-infested marsh and was camouflaged by drooping Spanish moss. Inside that shed, Charlie read the Good Book and mourned the loss of his wife, son, and world.

A year to the day after General Robert E. Lee's surrender at

Appomattox Court House, Charlie informed Susie-Jo he was ready to die. He told her he had lived a complete life. He had tasted glory and defeat; he had been through heaven and hell. He'd been righteous and shameful; he had sired life and taken it. Now, he was tired and tortured with grief, and he was getting itchy to join her mama. But before he passed through those Pearly Gates, he had one last feat to accomplish. He intended to make a pilgrimage to the Holy Land, for he wanted to gaze upon the River Jordan with his own eyes.

"Papa," Susie-Jo said, gently, "what are you talkin' about, honey? You know we can't go anywhere. Why, we don't have the money to buy a cow, let alone a journey to some A-rab nation. Be good now and finish up that bowl of rice."

Susie-Jo dismissed the notion from her mind, but Charlie thought of nothing else. He came to believe that the servants of Beelzebub were plotting to keep him out of Palestine, and his intention consequently morphed into a one-man crusade. He could smell the smoke of battle and hear the whiz of cannonballs, and he knew he would see the River Jordan for himself, or die trying.

"Susie-Jo" he said, pausing in his task of chopping up furniture for firewood one evening, "I'm a'gonna dig up the silver and buy us passage to the Holy Land."

"No, you're not, Papa," Susie-Jo told him, rolling her big, blue eyes. "You leave the family silver alone."

But Charlie didn't leave the silver alone. By the light of a fat May moon, he rolled over a boulder and dug deep in the sand beneath it. He uncovered a crate, secured it with ropes, and with all the straining might of Samson he hoisted it out of the reeking hole and up to fresh air. He pried the lid open and counted the familiar pieces. It was a collection of silver that once evoked envy at parties in the big house, but it was also a tangible history of his family's march through time. Some of the candlesticks dated back to the days of Charles-the-Second, and no less a person than President Jefferson Davis, himself, had put his blessed lips to the rim of a certain etched hunt cup. The silver collection was imbued with sentiment...and it would snatch a fetching sum from the Yankees. He sold the lot, and Susie-Jo soon found herself on the back of a dromedary.

Susie-Jo imagined that her papa would take one look at the Jordan River and keel over dead. That did not happen. Charlie's health and zeal were bolstered by his victory, so much so that he next insisted on following the course of the Jordan from the Sea of Galilee all the way down to the southern tip of the Dead Sea. This monumental expedition, which in Susie-Jo's mind rivaled the original exodus, only invigorated Charlie. He then expressed a desire to see the waters of the Negeb. His fellahin guides and his flabbergasted daughter objected mightily, but Charlie's tearful pleas brought them to heel. They climbed back on their camels and followed the Wadi al Jeib south, all the while baking under the merciless, middle-eastern sun.

A few days into this last excursion, they were overtaken by a raging sandstorm. The sand stung their faces raw and filled their ears, mouths, and nostrils. The camels refused to go on, and the party was stranded and lost on the Sinai Peninsula with no water or shelter in sight. It looked like the end, and so it was for everyone but Susie-Jo.

She never understood why she proved more robust than the rest. At the time, she could only watch helplessly as Charlie and the guides succumbed to dehydration and the elements. She came close to death herself, and was certain her prayers would be her last. Then a splash of water hit her in the face.

She tried to bring the images into focus, but the sand and the sun rendered her vision cloudy. Still, she managed to correctly deduce that a caravan had come along in the knick of time. The Bedouin tribesmen, speaking no English or schoolgirl French, revived her with water, fed her a cautious serving of lamb and laban, and soothed her sun blisters with ointment. They tied her onto yet another camel—a sad-eyed creature she named Beau. The caravan took three days and two nights to reach a desert camp south of Petra.

Susie-Jo, no stranger to change, now entered a world that shocked her at every turn. Exhausted and feeling she'd been sucked into a funhouse of exotic violations, she banished all memory and simply floated along as the moments presented themselves. She did not grieve for her parents; she did not grieve for her brother Joe-Joe; she did not even grieve for the South.

The men pulled her down from Beau and delivered her into the hands of their wives, who jabbered and bumped into one another like disturbed mud daubers. The wives shoved Susie-Jo into a tent. They stripped her of her western clothes and threw them into the fire. They began flapping their tongues and gobbling, which scared her so badly she peed. They scrubbed her, oiled her, and made her climb into a heavy, black get-up that covered every inch of her skin. It came with a matching veil that stole her easy breath and chains that swung in front of her eyes. Once the garb was on her, she too began to bump into everything and everyone. The wives guided her body by pushing it this way and that and poking it everywhere.

Late that evening, they pulled her outside and abandoned her at the entrance to a large tent. Two turbaned guards, carrying curved swords, peeled back the flaps and shouted at her in Arabic. She held out her arms and stepped blindly forward with tentative, baby steps. Impatient, the guards seized her and tossed her head first into the tent. She pulled herself up on her knees to behold a devilishly handsome sheik.

Although he was only twenty-six, Sheik Hamd Abu Fassal al-Mansaf exuded power. His body was lean, muscular, and at its prime. His dark eyes were sphinx-like in their mystery, and his thick, coral lips seemed poised to launch sarcasm. He lounged in a bright white Kuffiyyah on a throne made entirely of pillows. His ten sons—the oldest being seven—respectfully knelt at his pampered, naked feet.

"What is that?" he asked the captain of his guards in Arabic, as he pointed a slender, gold-ringed finger at Susie-Jo.

"It's that woman they found dying in the desert," the captain answered. "They thought maybe you would have her as your slave or concubine."

"Is she lovely?"

"Beautiful, but bizarre." The captain lowered his chin, tightened his lips, and wobbled his head. "I'm told, Your Highness, that these Europeans have no salt in their blood."

"So what? What does that mean? I don't want to cook her, you idiot!" Sheik Hamd sat up and clapped his hands twice. "Remove the veil!"

The guards did, and Susie-Jo's golden ringlets joyously sprang from their prison. Such light-colored hair frightened the Bedouin men. They gasped and carried on as though they were looking at Medussa. They warned one another not to look into her blue eyes, and they cowered while she was stripped and checked for deformities. They marveled at her white, jumbo moons, and discussed whether or not to put tassels on the tips of them. When they were satisfied that she had no gills or stinger, they ordered her to dress and modestly turned their heads as she did so.

"She is too proud to be a slave," complained Sheik Hamd. He sneaked a peek at Susie-Jo using his gem-encrusted dagger as a mirror, and he was amused to catch her sticking out her tongue at him. "Yes, far too proud."

"Once again, Your Highness, you have proven yourself to be an excellent judge of women," the captain said. "I agree. The woman is spoiled and is of no use. Let's kill her."

"I think not," Sheik Hamd told him. "I think I shall take her for a wife."

"But, Your Highness!"

"What? What now?"

"You already have six wives, Your Highness."

"I don't like the number six," said Sheik Hamd. He lazily stretched across his throne and closed his eyes. "Seven is a holy number."

Poor Susie-Jo. It seemed she was born under an unlucky star. She was forced to marry Sheik Hamd, and she went to his bed. Because she was his seventh wife, she was expected to labor as a household servant. The other wives kept her busy from dawn to dusk. They showed her how to weave their fancy rugs, how to bake shrak over flaming pits, and how to pack up camp at a moment's notice.

She hated her conjugal duties in the beginning, but she soon got over that hump. Turned out, Sheik Hamd was an indefatigable machine of pleasure. Susie-Jo eventually got hooked and couldn't get enough of the man, but that didn't stop her from trying. Many a night the camp awoke to her Rebel yells.

However, the bliss of the marriage bed did not make up for the drudgery of her daily existence. The other wives hated her, and they accused her of hogging the sheik to herself. They delighted in devising ways to torture her. They put maggots in her rice pudding and sand in her sour-milk sauce. They suspended her by her ankles over the edge of a crag, and they pantomimed skits that mocked and exaggerated her breast size. If it hadn't been for the loving arms of her potentate Romeo, she would have wandered off into the desert to reclaim the peaceful death the nomads had stolen from her.

On a night when the fourth wife was summoned to service Sheik Hamd, Susie-Jo was feeling sorry for herself in her tent when she was startled to hear her Christian name called. She lifted up the flap and looked out, but all she could see was Beau. The camel was forever chewing through his tether to roam free throughout the camp, so she whispered a rebuke to him, closed the flaps, and thought no more about it...that is, until Beau began to kick the side of her tent.

"I declare!" she hollered. "Stop all that kicking!"

"Get up and come out, Susie-Jo," insisted Beau. "I want to take you for a ride."

"I'm not goin' anywhere," she replied. "It's the middle of the night and... Huh? Wait a minute. Camels aren't supposed to talk!" She went outside and glared into his doleful eyes. "Were you or were you not just talking?"

"I were," he admitted.

"Well, if you plan to make a habit of it, you'll have to get some help with that grammar. A camel talkin'! I never heard tell of such a thing. Never imagined! But then again, I never imagined I'd be one of seven wives to a horny, A-rab sheik. So, what can I do for you, Beau?"

The dromedary lowered his hump and said "Get on." Susie-Jo straddled him and held onto his coarse hair, and he took off across the desert at a lumbersome canter. The sky was clear, the stars were bright, and the moon-dappled dunes shifted and sifted, casting off their dust to be carried away on the arid breeze. The splendor of the night inspired a psalm from Beau, the beauty of which moved Susie-Jo to tears. When they had traveled three miles or more, Beau screeched to a halt in front of a cave and told Susie-Jo to dismount and enter.

"Are you loony?" she asked him, placing her palms on the small of her back. "I'm supposed to go into that cave alone?"

"You got it." Beau yawned and settled down for a nap. "Primordial spaces give me the jitters, but don't let that stop you." He shut his eyes and yawned again. "There's nothing in there to harm you. Only a bottle and a ge...zzzzzzzZZZ."

"Stupid camel," Susie-Jo commented to herself, as Beau's snores shook the earth. "I can't believe he brought me all this way to pick up some da-burn bottle."

She squared her shoulders, took a huff, and entered the cave. It was intensely dark, and she had to feel her way along the cold and slimy walls. The ground was crunchy with what she took to be sand and booby-trapped with shin-splintering stalagmites. The gurgle of water and the shrieks of bats echoed through the dank chambers. Susie-Jo was about ready to hightail it out of there when her foot brushed against an object and set it rolling down an incline. Its course was halted by a rock, and her mind identified the "toink" of fine enamel. She groped along the cave floor, seized upon the bottle, and began to trace her fingers over its detailed surface.

As she held the bottle, a light began to throb from within it—faintly at first, then enough to bathe her hands in radiance. She was suddenly fearful and set the bottle down, but it glowed all the more. The entire cave was soon flooded with a strange luminescence, and Susie-Jo realized that she stood, not upon sand, but upon diamonds. It had not been water gurgling, but a trickling stream of melted gold. The stalagmites were actually huge blocks of rubies and emeralds, and the bats were not shrieking at all, but producing squeaks as they spit-polished sapphire stones.

Susie-Jo didn't dawdle in wonderment. Deciding there was a mystery afoot, she determined to solve it. She picked up the bottle and pulled the cork from its mouth. An eruption of light, dust, and wind whooshed from the bottle, knocking Susie-Jo off her feet. The particles swirled up and spun like a funnel, fearsome in power. Slowly, the dust and light began to coagulate into fat. Blobs of blubber flopped about spasmodically. Bones emerged from the sucking mass and muscles sprouted and climbed up the skeleton. Skin formed in patches until the complete body of a genie was formed.

And what a genie he was. He was as blue as a cornflower and as shiny as yellow squash. He had beady eyes; a drooping, black mustache; a hairy back; and a prizefighter's nose. His turban was dripping with pearls, and his pantaloons were spun of gold. He had cymbals on his fat fingers, and tiny bells on his toes. Diamonds sparkled from his earlobes and nostrils, and a ruby was tucked into his belly button.

"Praise Mecca!" he bellowed. "I've been in that bottle since the late-Umayyad period!"

"How long ago was that?" asked Susie-Jo.

"If you don't know, I'm certainly not going to tell you," the genie said, then sniffed. "I've always been sensitive about my age. My name's Baba Ali Roo. What's your's?"

"Susie-Jo Pickett-Smith Fassal al-Mansaf."

"Well, Susie-Jo," said Baba Ali Roo, with a bow, "thank you for releasing me. In exchange, I will grant you a wish."

"Only one?" asked Susie-Jo. "I'm supposed to get three, aren't I? That's what it says in all the books."

"I don't know..." Baba Ali Roo flexed a foot to stretch the muscles up the back of his leg. "Three wishes for pulling a cork out of a bottle? I'd call that excessive."

"You'd better make it three, mister," threatened Susie-Jo, "or my one wish will put you back in that bottle for another century or two."

"Ah!" Baba Ali Roo paused to smack his lips. "I guess some of you blondes do have brains. Very well, three wishes. Let me guess: tall, dark, and handsome, right?"

"I want to go home to South Carolina," Susie-Jo told him, firmly. "I want to be with my own people."

"Your wish is my command, Mistress."

With colossal effort, the genie wrestled a flying carpet from the narrow-lipped bottle. They sat cross-legged upon it and went whizzing across Arabia, the Mediterranean, and the stormy, gray Atlantic. Less than a week later, they flew over the spire of St. Michael's Parish in Charleston, and reached the old plantation that same afternoon.

Susie-Jo found everything worse than she left it. The grasses and vines completely covered her mother's grave and the ruins of the big house. The fishing shed was now the domain of some feisty-looking rattlers, and the rice plants were killed off by a late frost. More than half of the gentlefolk in the county had expired, so there were no more balls or parties to attend. It was a place for ghosts, and she was sure that her ancestors would be fine there alone.

"I want to go home," she said to Baba Ali Roo, a week after their arrival.

"You are home, Mistress," the genie reminded her.

"No, I want to go home to the desert." She brushed away a tear. "I want to be with my own people."

"Your wish is my command, Mistress."

Susie-Jo had a joyful homecoming at the camp. Beau wept with relief, and Sheik Hamd intoned his thanksgivings. Even the other wives were happy to see her return, for without her to bully, they had bickered with one another. Sheik Hamd called for a feast, and three lambs were slaughtered. After the men stuffed themselves at the celebratory mansaf, Susie-Jo helped herself to the plentiful leftovers. She was almost happy, but one thing still annoyed her.

"I have one more wish," she whispered to Baba Ali Roo, as the purple pall of night fell.

"Yes, I know," snapped the genie, his nerves raw because he was carpet-lagged. "Well, what is it?"

She told him what she wanted, and he nodded. But before he could answer with his customary, "Your wish is my command," the guards came and seized Susie-Jo. They took her to Sheik Hamd, who eagerly awaited her. He embraced her, kissed her, and promised that, thenceforth, she would be his only lover. He told her everything she could ever hope to hear from a man, and her breasts were moistened by his earnest tears. As she melted into his strong arms and surrendered to his powerful, spiced aroma, she turned her head and muttered, "I thank you, dear Baba Ali Roo."

Chapter 10

ERICH AND THE WEREWOLF

E CAME HOME TO HER IN MID-MARCH, ON A SATURDAY. THE cold winds whipped across the east-Elbian plains, and ice lay in the potato fields. The Baroness was in the study, rebuking the estate-inspector Fritz, when she heard the chapel bells ringing, and she knew in her heart that her husband was near. She grabbed her fur coat and rushed out of the manor. In a moment, Lothar came galloping up the birch-lined lane.

"Johanna, Liebchen," he said, reaching down from his saddle. "How good it is to be home."

"Lothar!" cried the Baroness. She grasped his gloved hand and held it to her cheek. "How long are you staying? As long as a week?"

"Perhaps."

Colonel Lothar von Stehlenberg was a handsomely chiseled man in his early thirties. He stood more than six-feet tall with white-blond hair and steel-gray eyes. A dueling scar ran from the middle of his left cheek to his ear, but such a mark was prized in the militaristic kingdom of Prussia. The Colonel, like most of his men, was formal, disciplined, and taut. A conscientious man, he strove for perfection. He had simple, tidy tastes; he was never showy; and his Lutheran piety was as renowned as his frugality and martial skill. The army was his life, although a piece of him was always called back to Schäfleinheim, his ancestral estate.

"How is little Erich?" he asked, dismounting. He gave the reins to a Polish peasant, who led the horse to the stables.

Lothar's question was poignant. It brought to both their minds not only their five-year-old tyke in the nursery but also his older brother Lothar, nicknamed 'Der Baum', meaning 'the tree'. And they could not summon forth the memory of Der Baum's sweet face without recalling his horribly gruesome end. Their eyes involuntarily darted to the dwarf apple tree and the ice-covered grave beside it.

"Erich is wonderful!" Johanna insisted, forcefully, to drive back their agony. She laughed and playfully took her husband's arm. "Each day, I say he looks more and more like my Colonel. I am so proud. He even gives orders like you. Ha-ha! Wait until he has a scar!"

They seemed the luckiest of couples, this dashing officer and his blond, plump-cheeked wife. They were the epitome of everything that was comely and seemly. Their superiors, friends, and minister agreed that hands like theirs would secure a unified Deutschland. What people said mattered little, however, because Lothar and Johanna were unable to secure the safety of their own home.

Upstairs in the nursery, the nanny Helga and her Polish maid Krystyna were hurriedly dressing Erich in a cavalry uniform. The child had all the physical beauty of his parents, but none of their restraint. He was stubborn and mischievous, and Helga regularly resorted to beating him. She felt it her duty in the absence of the Colonel. She felt a strong hand was needed when rebellion reared its ugly head. She was convinced of it, being the first trainer of many a von Stehlenberg officer in her day. No one dared question her methods, since she always achieved the desired goal—an obedient, courageous German.

"Erich, kommen Sie her!" she said, clamping her dentures to keep them from flying. She yanked the child to her and smacked his backside. "A baron's son never squirms!"

"I am not going to wear that silly helmet," Erich defiantly told her. "It doesn't fit."

"But young Master!" the maid Krystyna pleaded, as she polished the helmet with her apron. "You must put it on, else the effect will be lost and your father will—"

"Ja, ja," he relented, to shut her up. "One day, when I am baron, I will cease to listen to servant women."

"Hel-ga!" shouted Johanna, from the bottom of the old staircase. "Bring Erich down! His father wants to see him!"

Helga beat out a cadence on a tin drum, and Erich marched down to greet his father. He halted before him, clicked his heels, and saluted. He removed his oversized helmet and tucked it under his arm.

"Are you well, Soldier?" Lothar asked, bending to get a good look at him. "Stick out your chest!"

"Zu Befehl!" answered Erich, careful to keep his 'Yes, Sir!' low-pitched and crisp.

"Bitte," Lothar said, standing erect. "You executed your maneuvers with precision and polish. Be at ease, and let us have a coffee and a bite of cake. I brought along fine coffee."

"How thoughtful of you, Lothar!" Johanna impulsively kissed his cheek and then stepped back to blush. "Coffee from Berlin!"

"Coffee from Africa, Leibchen, by way of Berlin. We mustn't have Erich thinking that coffee grows atop the Brandenburg Gate."

That night as the family slept, Krystyna stole out of the servants' wing into the smoke house, where her lover awaited. Slavo was a field hand and a brute. He greeted Krystyna with a bear hug, and probed her protesting mouth with his thick tongue.

"Don't groan so loud!" she hissed at him in Polish, when she'd managed to turn her head. "The master is home."

"The master can go to the devil," Slavo said, undoing the laces of her undergarments. "Hmmmm!"

"Slavo!" Krystyna pushed him off her and ran behind a hanging ham to gain a moment of freedom. "If they catch me with you, they will take me from the house and put me in the fields."

"Who cares?" Slavo grabbed for her but was slowed by the bulk of his muscles. She slipped by him easily, and he sighed with frustration. "It is better to toil in the honest earth than to coddle a German brat."

"Do you not produce food for their table?" snapped Krystyna. "Don't you grow hops for their beer, eh? I am only helping to see that this child does not fall into the hands of the werewolf. Is that so bad?"

"Werewolf!" Slavo laughed and rubbed his hairy belly. "You sound like an old Gypsy."

"You didn't see what little was left of the other son," she told him, her eyes wide with fear. "It was sickening. Only a werewolf could have done that."

"Or a mad German," added Slavo. "Come here, you minx. I'll be the big, bad wolf and eat you up. Grrr!"

The next morning, another horseman arrived at Schäfleinheim: Oberleutnant Karl von Stehlenberg, the Colonel's middle brother. Karl would not accept ale or sit down to Frühstück before giving an urgent report. A mob rioted in the Prussian capital, setting up barricades. Shots were exchanged, and corpses littered the palace square. The king refused to flee to safety, so General Prittwitz was recalling all officers on leave. Lothar must return to Berlin at once.

Without overtly showing affection, Lothar again left Johanna. She resumed the run of the manor and the tedious tasks of managing a large estate. Her duties were so numerous that she scarcely had time to think of the Colonel...or that thing. She was swamped with hiring hands, signing official papers, and the hysteria of squabbling house-maids. She relied on the estate-inspector Fritz and the bailiff Hermann to implement her orders.

Fritz and Hermann were Germans, and their families had long been in the service of the Barons von Stehlenberg. Like their ancestors, they had only contempt for the Poles. They thought of them as beasts and treated them as such. That spring, as news trickled in about the revolutions sweeping Europe, Fritz and Hermann took the opportunity to implement ever more draconian measures against the Poles. Any minor offense was punished by confinement or beating. A half-dozen peasant men were rounded up, accused of poaching, and hung from the limbs of an oak. The Poles bristled, and Slavo sought to rally them. He thought up a diabolical plan that would wreak vengeance on the Colonel and his henchmen, but it could not be done without Krystyna's help.

"That brat you wait upon; what's his name?" Slavo asked her, one night in the smokehouse.

"Erich?" Krystyna slipped back into her nightdress. "What about him?"

"He has his own room?"

"Of course, fool."

"Does he trust you? Obey you?"

"He prefers me to Helga, I can tell you that much." She lifted her dress to brush off her knees. "What are these questions? What do you want?" She did not wait for his answer, but turned to find her boots and leave.

"No, you're not going," Slavo said, rolling across the floor to her feet. He clutched her ankles and blew hot breath up her legs. "Let me have it again, then I will tell you what I need."

What Slavo needed was her complicity in a kidnapping. Krystyna was deeply distressed when he told her, but he said she'd have to do it or he would find another girl to satisfy him. Where, after all, was her patriotism? Wouldn't she sacrifice anything to help win a free Poland? He promised her he would not harm the boy—only hold him for ransom and buy guns with the money. Krystyna consented.

That May saw an outbreak of polio, and Johanna was brought news one morning that her sister Elsa lay on her deathbed. It was unthinkable that Johanna would do anything except rush to her brother-in-law's estate, which neighbored Schäfleinheim...and yet, she hesitated. She knew she could not risk exposing Erich to the polio, but did she dare part with him? She groaned and frantically paced. She was not sure if the foreboding she felt was a warning from Heaven or a tormenting lie from the Liar of Liars, forged to unnerve her and stop her from keeping a prayerful watch over her sister's passing. Elsa had always been dear to her. She deserved a proper adieu. Johanna relaxed a little when she made up her mind that there was really no choice to make. Kissing the white-blond hair on top of Erich's head, she reminded him that she would always love him and told him to mind Helga. Then she fled from the room before she began to cry. She would never again look upon her son.

Half an hour after the Baroness galloped across the potato fields and out of sight, Slavo crept up the servants' staircase to the nursery. While Krystyna distracted Erich with his tin soldiers, Slavo knocked Helga out with a swift jab of his fist to the side of her head. The old nanny's knees did not give, and she tipped and crashed to the floor. Erich put up fiery resistance, but he was no match for the field hand. Slavo rolled the writhing lad tightly in a rug and slung it over one of his broad Polish shoulders. Krystyna tied a ransom note around the neck of a hobbyhorse and shut the nursery door behind them. They were halfway down the stairs before it all went horribly wrong.

Fritz and Hermann had spent the morning working the field peasants. The weather was clear and unseasonably cold, but a warm front moved in before noon, bringing a thunderstorm with it. The two overseers decided to leave the peasants in the fields and head to the manor kitchens for their Mittagessen.

When the Poles tending the grounds and stables saw the Germans coming up the lane a full hour earlier than expected, they braced themselves for trouble. Slavo would surely be discovered and killed, and the rest of them would be subject to the usual interrogation, denial, and punishment. But this time, they decided to fight. Some boys were sent to collect a cache of pikes, and another ran to call the men from the fields.

Fritz and Hermann saw the mob gathering ahead of them. They took their shotguns from their saddles and cautiously continued toward the kitchens, calling out to the peasants and warning them not to do anything foolish. An old woman threw a stone that bounced off Fritz's forehead. Shots rang out, and blood began to spill.

Slavo carried Erich out the back of the manor and across the eastern fields, towards the forest. Krystyna struggled to keep abreast, but her skirts grew heavy with mud. She fell and screamed. Fritz heard her and pursued. He struck Krystyna in the back of her neck with the butt of his shotgun, killing her instantly. He then shot Slavo in the leg, and he was reloading to finish the job when a Pole sent a bullet boring through Fritz's brain. Slavo stumbled into the woods with Erich.

A few days later, several miles to the east, a Polish woman was picking mushrooms in the forest. She was an elderly peasant—a hag, really—who had much in common with the Speisemorchel she gathered into her small wheelbarrow. As a girl, she was ravaged by smallpox, and her face was now a battlefield of craters, wrinkles, warts, and sores. Her eyelids, cheeks, and breasts sagged, and her knees and feet were swollen. She had hardly any teeth, and her nose was wide and bubbled. The babushka on her head was stained with the soot of her smoking fireplace, and her woolen skirts were picked and smelled of bacon. Strips of yellowed bandages wound around each of her hands, leaving her fingers free for business; and army-issue boots, gleaned from a scene of carnage, kept her feet nice and dry.

She was blithely harvesting—wailing out the mournful melody of a Polish folk song—when she stepped upon the stinking corpse of a man. She saw the maggot-infested wound in his leg and concluded that he had died in agony. She kissed the crucifix that hung about her neck and clucked her tongue. Although she wasn't strong enough to bury him, she was alive enough to make use of his rug. When she went to pick it up, however, out rolled a boy. He was fevered and delirious, but breathing. She managed to get him into her wheelbarrow, and she took him home.

The hag's cottage, which sat nestled in a cluster of giant spruce, was humble but colorfully stenciled. Squirrels hopped across its grassy roof, and a grimalkin bathed by the well. Inside, a kettle of broth simmered over the smoky fire, and a pudding steamed in a pot beside the grate. Dried herbs hung from the ceiling beams, and a statue of the Blessed Virgin stood guard beside the only window.

As best she could, the old woman tucked the blond boy into her bed and nursed him for days. He tossed and turned, and he sweated and coughed. He was tortured by nightmares and often called out through his fever. The woman spoke little German, but she managed to decipher a few words. "Werewolf" was one of them.

Mostly, though, he shouted out, "Zu Befehl!" so she began to call him Zu. His fever broke on the fourth night, and he gained a peaceful sleep. The next morning, he sat up, drank a bowl of broth, and ate a piece of black bread. His appetite returned, but his memory did not.

"Who are you?" she asked him in Polish, as he rocked in a chair by the fire. He stared at her in innocent astonishment, and it melted her heart. The boy was lost in the world—lost to his self. She would claim him as her own—for the moment—so that he would have a rock upon which to stand. "Your name is Zu," she said, hugging him, "and I am your Mamuska."

"Ma-muuu-ska," repeated Zu.

She wanted to return the boy to his mother—if he had a living mother—but she was too old and weak to travel any real distance. She suffered from chills night and day, and her feet would never carry her to the nearest town. Her trap needed a wheel, and her donkey was depressed. There was nothing she could do, except keep the boy and love him. She began to teach him all she knew about the world, and he quickly grasped the elementals of the Polish language.

The snows fell early that year, and travel to and from the cottage became impossible. Mamuska and Zu amused themselves with games and rabbit stew. They came to care for each other as mother and son, and their laughter rang out on the worst of winter nights.

One day, Mamuska realized that she was dreading the spring thaw, for she no longer wanted to return Zu to his mother. He was as honey to her bitter bread, and she could not bear to part with him. So she did a wicked thing. Remembering his nightmares, she told him the forest was full of werewolves who ate little boys. She warned him never to speak to anyone but her.

"These are clever werewolves," she said in a quivering voice. "They look like you or me because they are hairy only on the inside, unless it is a full moon. But when the moon is round and high above the earth, their ugly natures are made manifest, and their hunger will be satisfied. So beware, my child! Beware!"

Zu believed her absolutely, and his nightmares resumed. During the day, werewolves haunted his imagination. He thought he saw them lurking behind trees or hiding in the branches. He was sure he saw one looking in the window one night after supper, but Mamuska assured him it was the wind in the trees.

Another time he believed he saw a werewolf. It was a July afternoon, hot and sticky. The wind had dropped, the birds were singing, and the insects were humming, buzzing, and chirruping. He was whittling by the open window when Mamuska rushed into the cottage and barred the door behind her. He had never seen her move so adroitly.

"Quick!" she shouted, pulling him by his shirt. "A werewolf is coming! He will eat you if he sees you! We must hide you in the cupboard!"

"But what about you, Mamuska?"

"He will not eat me. I am too disfigured. Now, hurry! Don't make a peep!"

Zu did not make a peep, but he took one. Ever so quietly, ever so slightly, he opened the cupboard door and peeped through the crack. His eyes widened, and his mouth fell slack.

A tall man with white-blond hair stood on the cottage threshold. His clothes were bright and handsome, with golden cords and colorful ribbons. His trousers had red stripes down the outside legs, and his black-leather boots were glossy. He spoke poor Polish, though he seemed cordial enough. Zu thought there was something vaguely familiar about this werewolf, and he would have liked to speak with him. It was not to be, for Mamuska gave the werewolf some bread, wished him luck, and sent him on his way.

The years passed, the donkey died, and Mamuska grew more stiff in her joints. By his twenty-sixth birthday, Zu was doing all the chores, including the cooking and washing. He was a handsome man: quite tall, with chiseled features and steel-gray eyes. His mind was quick, and his good humor was ready; but in terms of the world at large, he was a simpleton.

He was setting up a bear trap one foggy October day, when he caught sight of a fawn nibbling on the bark of a tree. He was enchanted by her grace and followed her as she progressed. The fog thickened, and he lost her. He turned to retrace his steps, and a werewolf stepped from behind a hazelnut tree.

"Guten Morgan!" the werewolf called out, smugly. He was wearing a long, black cape and thigh-high boots. His hair was silver at his temples, but his skin was pink and unlined. He smiled, revealing a row of gleaming-white, sharp teeth, and he took off his kid gloves to expose his exquisitely manicured fingernails. He clicked his heels, executed a snappy bow, and said, in Polish, "I am Count Wolfgang Wilhelm von Lehn."

"You are a werewolf!" cried Zu, pointing his finger. "You stay away from me!"

"You have something against werewolves?" asked the Count. "I am sorry to hear it. I hoped we could be friends."

"Friends?" Zu shook his head. "You want to eat me!"

"You do look tasty," the Count admitted, "but I am a creature of self- restraint. I am Prussian."

"What?"

"Never mind," said the Count, aghast. "I've gotten myself lost in the forest. My horse went lame, you see, and I had to shoot the troublesome thing. I'm afraid you'll have to put me up for the night. I want to make a fresh start of it tomorrow morning."

"Oh no," Zu told him, "that won't do. My Mamuska would never allow a werewolf to..."

"To what? To eat some revolting sausage and schmand and get a good night's sleep? Your Mamuska sounds formidable, not to say inhospitable. Friend, I beseech you to... What is your name?"

"Zu."

"Zu?" The Count swung his gloves around once, in a circle, and pursed his lips. "What an interesting name. Well, Zu, why should you or your Mamuska be worried? The moon will not be full tonight. I will be harmless. Go tell the woman to take pity on a wayfarer."

Against her better judgment, Mamuska permitted the Count a night's stay in her cottage. She could hardly refuse a Prussian aristocrat, for to do so would mean certain reprisal. She did not believe he was a werewolf—she did not really believe in werewolves—but she thought a werewolf would have been a preferable guest.

"You are the very image of an acquaintance of mine," the Count told Zu, as Mamuska cleared their bowls. "You have his coloring and nose. Oddly enough, your lips are like his wife's. Ah, Johanna! The Baroness was a splendid-looking woman."

"Was?" asked Zu. "What happened to her?"

"She hung herself from an apple tree."

"This unlucky talk," protested Mamuska, and she crossed herself. "Let us speak of other things."

"Wait, I want to hear." Zu dared to pull his chair a bit closer to the Count's. "Why did the Baroness kill herself?"

"Some Poles made off with her only surviving son. She'd lost her firstborn to fever, so they say, though the boy's death was cloaked in mystery. Then came 'forty-eight, the year of troubles. There was an uprising on the Baron's estate. It was easily put down, but the second son was missing. For ten years, Johanna clung to hope. And then...she blamed herself, you see."

"It is not fitting to talk like this before bed," Mamuska insisted. "We will have nightmares. Come let us get some sleep. Count von Lehn may have the bed, and Zu and I will curl up by the fire."

Mamuska did not sleep well. She was certain that Zu was the poor Baroness' son, and she was also sure the Count knew the truth. The anguish of it tore through her brain for hours, like a wild boar rooting up fungi of fear. She decided she would rise early, and somehow get the Count on his way and out of their lives. But as the woodpeckers began their morning work, Mamuska fell into a deep sleep. When she awoke, she found she had overslept and that the men were dressed and fed. She rolled onto her back and saw Zu standing above her. She smiled at him...and he spat on her.

"You vile witch!" he screamed, kicking her in the ribs. "Did you think I would never find out? Did you think my memories would never return? You liar!"

"Wait! I can explain, Zu!"

"Don't call me that!" He backed away, and tears of anger streamed down his cheeks. "I am Erich von Stehlenberg! If you had delivered me to my mother, she would be alive today! I trusted you!"

"Zu, please!"

"Errrrr-iiiiich!" he roared, his eyes wild with emotion. "Erich! Erich! Erich!"

"Bitte," said the Count, stepping forward. "There's no need for unpleasantness. I am returning Erich to his people. He never wants to see you again, old hag. There, that's simple enough, isn't it?" He turned on his heel and said, in German, "Come along, Erich."

Mamuska followed the men out of the cottage. She slipped on some wet pine needles, and the Count laughed at her. In spite of the stabbing pain in her ribs, she called out to her Zu and continued to do so, long after he was gone.

Erich and the Count found their way to the nearest village, where they caught a coach to a bigger village, where the Count purchased a horse, and the two of them set off in one saddle for Schäfleinheim. The closer he got to home, the more Erich remembered of his early years. He wept on the back of the Count's shoulder when an image of his mother came to his mind. He saw her clearly, in a nursery, and she was as pretty as an angel. How he wished she had lived to witness his homecoming!

It was now late autumn. The potato fields were burned off, and a light mist softened the soil. There was pheasant hunting at Schäfleinheim, and the thuds of the guns could be heard from quite a distance.

Count von Lehn carefully guided the horse out of a thicket by a lake. Waving his cape, he called for a halt. The beaters echoed the call, and the guns ceased. With Erich alone in the saddle, the Count walked the horse down the path, towards the shooting party.

The hunters were a sophisticated lot, most of them on holiday from Berlin or Posen. They were, without exception, excellent marksmen. They were, without exception, Prussian aristocrats. They knew their own, and despite Erich's rugged apparel and appearance, they instantly recognized him to be the long lost son of Lothar and Johanna. They groaned as the awful truth hit them.

"Mein Gott!" exclaimed a field marshal's wife, grasping the arm of her lover, the field marshal's nephew. "Wolfgang has raised the dead!"

"So it would appear," her lover said dryly, as he broke open his shotgun to inspect the barrel. "I'm afraid this won't be perceived as good news by his male cousins."

The field marshall's wife popped a monocle into one eye and squinted the other. "His hair is long like an artist's, and he's wearing... Polish clothes. Oh, dear. He'll have to be scrubbed pink."

"Why today?" whined her lover. "The shooting was extraordinary. Now we'll have to halt everything for some appalling scene of sentiment."

Sentiment is a relative term, especially in East Prussia. When Lothar von Stehlenberg, now General, saw his son, he grunted, embraced him stiffly, and then rode off to sit by Johanna's grave. He rejoined the party in the manor that evening, as composed as ever.

In the following months, no effort was spared to expedite the reassimilation of Erich into his pack. He spent his mornings with tutors and books. He studied mathematics and some history, but particular care was given to the German language. All Polish words were forbidden him, and so was any talk of his past. The family's minister worked to eradicate any hint of Catholicism or peasant superstition, and a valet was brought from Berlin to steer Erich through the days and coach him in matters of form. An army career was, alas, out of the question, but it was still necessary for Erich to be drilled in military exercises, simply to move with self-respect in martial, Junker society. On Tuesdays and Thursdays, he went to the fields to study agriculture, and he delighted in watching the turning of the soil and the coaxing of nature.

The General remained distant, spending little time at Schäfleinheim. When he was home, he was polite to his son but never effusive. An emotionally inaccessible man, the tragedies on his home-front had driven him to complete detachment. He fell, the following September, at the battle of Sedan. His body was brought home on a stormy Friday. In accordance with his will, he was buried beneath the dwarf apple tree, alongside Johanna and their firstborn.

With his father dead and his uncles and cousins at war, Erich turned to Count von Lehn for council. The Count was happy to oblige. He left his own dwindling estate and took a room at Schäfleinheim. He soon made himself indispensable to Erich, who, as the new baron, was awash in responsibilities. The two men became great friends and spent all their time together. Erich began to absorb the Count's view of the world, a view that was urbane, cynical, and yet darkly romantic.

"It is good that your parents are dead," the Count said to Erich, as they sat lavishly dining one evening. "A man is but a prisoner while his parents live. They will continually check his power and thwart his desires. Consider yourself fortunate. You are Siegfried! You are Faust! You are master!"

"Beware of women," he advised, another time. "Enjoy them, yes, but then discard them. And do not marry—or if you must, do it late in life, after you've accomplished something grand. Otherwise, a wife will drag you down to mediocrity."

"Do you ever think of the old Pole?" he asked Erich between bites of Kirshtorte, as they sat in a café during a visit to Berlin. "You mustn't. She is nothing to man or Heaven. A hag and no more. Dismiss those memories from your mind or they will weaken you. Remember, you are Barbarossa! You are Frederich-the-Great!"

These words and innumerable ones like them were delivered with such conviction and theatricality that Erich swallowed them whole without discretion. He was sucked into a vortex of "Sturm and Drang" and seduced by heady notions of his own superiority. The Count entertained and flattered him, and Erich basked in the glow. There was only one thing he didn't like about the Count—he was a werewolf.

Every full moon Erich would chain the Count to the walls of the wine cellar, and the baying would last through the night. The Count, in his wolf state, was insatiable. He would stop at nothing to get his meal of meat. Erich would throw a lamb or calf to the shackled beast, and upon returning in the morning, he would find the farm animals reduced to hoof, bone, and hide or wool. Then he would take the sobbing Count and bathe him, and they would not speak of it again until the next full moon. This was a messy business, and it aroused suspicion. Erich's female relatives fled to the capital, and the Polish peasants, who had nowhere else to go, murmured.

It was early the next February when news reached Schäfleinheim that Wilhelm-the-First had been proclaimed emperor of a united Germany. To celebrate, Erich opened a bottle of schnapps, and he and the Count began to drink...and drink. They passed out, and the full moon rose. In the morning, the old nanny Helga was discovered half eaten beside the spore of a large wolf. The peasants did not mourn her passing, but they were frightened. Holding torches and pitchforks, they stormed the manor and burned it to the ground. Erich and the Count escaped into the woods.

The two men survived on winterberries and hares for nearly a month. They were unable to return home because the accusations of the peasants could all too easily be proven true—the Count was a werewolf, and Erich was his accomplice. They decided to move eastward through the forest until they reached the Russian territories. They agreed they would go as far as St. Petersburg to begin a new life. But it was not to be.

They had built their fire and skinned their hare one cold night, when a full moon rose high and white over the treetops. They noticed it at the same time and looked at each other, nervously. "Hmm," said the Count, but Erich said nothing. He did, however, make certain that the Count got more than half the hare. It didn't help. Less than an hour after they'd finished eating, the Count began to thrash about in a violent fit. Long, coarse hairs sprouted all over his body; his nails grew and split open the fingers of his kid gloves; his nose popped and crackled as it stretched into a snout; a feral musk seeped from the pores of his loins; and his chest expanded to burst through his shirt and waistcoat. He scratched behind his ear with his foot and howled at the moon. Then he licked his salivating chops and came towards Erich.

"Nein!" shouted Erich. He shook off his inertia and tore off into the deep forest. "Help me!" he cried, as he ran.

But there was none to hear his pleas, and the werewolf gained on him. He'd gone perhaps a mile when he stumbled upon the old Polish woman's cottage. He had no time to be surprised, merely time to beat upon the door. As he did, the werewolf sunk his teeth into Erich's shoulder and shook violently.

"Help me!"

Mamuska was now nearing ninety, but the sound of her Zu's distress stirred her to quick action. Mustering all the energy she had within her, she grabbed an axe and threw open the door. She struck off one of the werewolf's paws, and blood spattered onto her face. The werewolf yelped and recoiled in agony. Mamuska yanked Erich inside the cottage and barred the door.

"Zu!" she wept, falling to the floor to hold him next to her bosom. "My Zu!"

"Ma-mus-ka?"

"Yes, it is I, my darling boy!" The old woman smiled through her tears as Erich's blood pumped out of him. "Mamuska is here."

"I'm going to become a werewolf," he told her in Polish.

"No, the wound is too severe for that," she assured him. "Don't worry. You are only going to die."

"Mamuska?"

"Yes, darling?"

"I'm sorry for..."

"Don't," she said, placing her finger over his lips. "There is no need. Mamuska loves you."

"I love you, too," he said, and died.

Chapter 11

ARCHIBALD AND SANTA CLAUS

RCHIBALD MACTAVISH—INVESTMENT BANKER, INDUSTRIALIST, and champion of laissez-faire capitalism—was nearly killed outside a Broadway theatre one night. The bullet missed him by inches. At the time, he affected nonchalance, because a crowd formed and the press was swarming. He later recalled the assassination of President William McKinley, two years before, and he couldn't help thinking that America had gone mad. Successful men were no longer admired, but resented. The anarchists were everywhere—one never knew. In Archibald's case, the perpetrator happened to be a woman...and a mother.

It was a damnable year for Archibald from start to finish. He had made money, to be sure, but not as much as the previous year. The so-called "Progressive Movement" had wreaked havoc with production in his utility, textile, and mining companies, and that Teddy Roosevelt had stirred up the national press about monopolies.

One journalist in particular—a skinny hellcat named Gertrude Moore—had latched onto Archibald as the chief subject of her copy. In article after article she publicly challenged him to provide higher pay and shorter hours for his workers. Archibald considered the woman a complete nuisance. She whipped the liberals into a froth, and for no good reason. After all, he told himself and anyone listening, his workers toiled twelve-hour days at ten cents an hour, the same as any laborers across America. If an employee wanted a better life, he could take the initiative to create it for himself, as Archibald had done.

This glib defense was sorely put to the test by two accidents. First, there was that terrible fire at his undergarment factory, back home in Boston, followed by the Thanksgiving Day cave-in of his West Virginia mine. The woman with the gun lost her only son in that mine. He died a week short of his seventeenth birthday. It was tragic, Archibald agreed, but hardly a reason to go about shooting at a man, especially a man so vital to the United States economy.

What annoyed him most about the shooting incident was that he hadn't wanted to go to the theatre—at least not that theatre. Highbrow nonsense, that's what the show sounded like to him. He said so to Tilly that morning, before he purchased their tickets.

"Highbrow nonsense!" he bellowed, with shaving cream on his jaw line and a Cuban cigar poking out from beneath his walrus mustache. "Confound it, I don't care to see Lillie Langtry in some gloomy play about divorce! Let's go see Diamond Lil', instead."

"No," was Tilly's reply, from under the pink, satin sheets.

"Why not?"

"Because I don't like that Lillian Russell."

"Why not?"

"Because her boobies are bigger than mine."

"That's why I wanna see 'em!"

Archibald belly-flopped onto the bed and playfully spanked her. She giggled, and they tumbled about for a bit. Then she pulled away, pursing her lips into a Cupid's bow.

"You can't fool me, Archie. You don't wanna take me to the fancy play 'cause you're scared you'll run into your pals. Ain't that the truth? Huh?"

"Tilly, tootsie, we wouldn't want my wife to discover our little secret, would we?"

"Aw, she probably already knows, if she's got any sense. What's she like, anyhow?"

"Who, Eleanor?" Archibald stood to wipe his face and fetch his cigar. "Eleanor is like any other Boston Brahmin, I suppose. A product

132

of her upbringing."

"Yeah? How so? Give me an example."

"Well, let's see…she reads too much, for one thing."

"What does she read?"

"Lots of gobbledygook," he mumbled, attaching his fresh, white collar to his shirt. "She reads Hawthorne, Longfellow, Emerson…all those dry, dead, New England writers. And I'm sorry to say she's fond of Henry James."

"Golly, I ain't never heard of them fellas. I guess I ain't quality."

Archibald eventually took Tilly to see "Mrs. Deering's Divorce", and for his trouble, he'd almost been done in by that coal miner's mother. He was sure that Gertrude Moore would run a story about the shooting, and then the Boston papers would pick it up, and then he'd have to explain to Eleanor why he'd been escorting a red-haired floozy to the theatre. The news of his affair would grieve his wife, but he felt she only had herself to blame.

Eleanor didn't like New York. She preferred summers on Martha's Vineyard and the rest of her time in Boston. This meant that the couple lived separate lives, yet Eleanor never once expressed concern about her husband's recreation in Manhattan. She was so wrapped up in her books and charities that she didn't appear to need a man. But Archibald found he needed a woman.

The day came when he took a long look in the mirror and discovered a lonely, middle-aged reflection. It was then he decided to find a plump dumpling to spoil. He went down to Coney Island without his wedding ring and encountered Tilly selling caramel apples. They smooched on the Ferris wheel and frolicked under the pier. It was great, naughty fun and the first of many romps, but Tilly's allure proved fleeting. Archibald now tired of her. He knew it. She knew it. It couldn't be helped.

"Hey, Archie!" she had screeched that night in front of the theatre. "Somebody just tried to kill ya!"

"I know that!" he snapped, picking himself up from the pavement to dust off his tails and top hat. "Don't you think I know that?"

The incident did make the papers. Still, the brouhaha might have been far worse. There were, thank heaven, no illustrations. Gertrude Moore did mention Tilly. Her article did not give Tilly's name, only used the term "vixen." That was all right, thought Archie. It could even be good press. It would put some swagger into his strut. He only hoped his wife would see it that way.

As it turned out, Eleanor was, on the surface, cavalier about the whole matter. She never mentioned it directly. True to form, she remained aloof, composed, and elegant. When she did seek revenge, it was with premeditation and wit. She chose to exact her modest toll on Christmas Eve, when Archibald returned to the old house on Beacon Hill. After the couple took their sons Cabot and Albert to a candlelight service, the family sat down to a late-night supper of goose meat sandwiches and plum pudding, prepared by the servants. Then they moved into the drawing room to cozy up by the blazing hearth. Archibald poured himself a brandy, and they began opening their presents, which lay beneath the Christmas tree.

"Mommy!" squealed tiny Albert, who was but six. He was wearing a blue-velvet suit with short pants and knee socks. "For whom shall I pull a present?"

"Hm?" His mother looked at him, her eyes at half-mast. "Oh, do push that big one over to your father, dear. That's my special gift to him this Christmas."

Albert struggled with the heavy package, finally enlisting the help of his older brother Cabot. Archibald adjusted the box between his feet. His mustache twitched, and he rubbed his palms with enthusiasm. As he lifted the contents from the mass of paper, however, a quizzical look came over his face.

"It's a saddle," he said, deflated.

"Yes, dear. A well-crafted one."

"But it's a saddle."

"Yes, dear. A hunt saddle."

"Eleanor, you know I don't ride. You know very well that I am terrified of horses."

"Really, dear?" Eleanor raised an eyebrow. "It was my understanding that you'd recently taken up foxhunting."

That was all she said, but it was enough. It implied the word "vixen," and it was smug with judgment. Cabot and Albert gaped at Archibald. Without comprehending the specifics, they sensed that their father was guilty of some dastardly deed.

"What are you looking at?" he growled at them.

The family resumed their gift giving, but Archibald took his brandy, cigar, and saddle into the library and shut the doors. He set the saddle on his desk and glowered at the thing. The fact that the saddle had undoubtedly cost him a bundle only served to pain him more. Eleanor would never let him sell it. She meant it to be his albatross.

He sipped his brandy and sunk into self-loathing. He dwelt on his weaknesses, infidelity, and crimes. He thought of the hundreds of thousands of workers that were at his mercy. He thought of their wives and children, all living in squalid mill town duplexes and mining town shacks. He thought of Tilly living in a one-bedroom apartment. It seemed the workers, wives, children, and mistresses of this world were all without guile and that he alone had a soul stained with manipulation. Such were his thoughts when a knock at the door scattered them.

"Archibald?" Eleanor peeked in, then entered. "Archibald, for goodness sake, don't drink anymore tonight. You'll ruin the holidays if you take to moping."

"Have the boys gone off to bed?"

"Yes. I must say, Albert was disappointed you neglected to open his gift. He made you something, specially. You'll have to make it up to him in the morning." She turned to go, then flowingly returned. "Oh, you won't forget to set up Albert's toys, will you? You've already hurt him once. I want him to have a good Christmas Day."

Eleanor left the library, leaving a wake of guilt behind her. Archibald plunged in, bemoaning the fact that he would not be remembered as an all-around nice guy. He thought that his epitaph would likely read, "Son of a bitch." If only he could reform himself. If only he could be the disgustingly sweet saint people seemed to want. If only he had a new heart. If only...

He stuck his cigar in his mouth and went back into the drawing room. The room smelt of pine and the bitter smoke of tree candles, recently extinguished. He turned up the gaslights and set about the task of assembling Albert's toys. No sooner did he finish, than a great commotion erupted from the fireplace. He turned about to see Santa Claus hastily slapping out sparks on his backside.

"Ho! Ho! Ho!" the old fellow said, with sarcasm. "I suppose you thought it would be funny to set Santa's butt on fire? I'll thank you to keep this chimney cold next year, Archibald MacTavish!"

"You know my name?"

"When I care to use it." Santa opened his bag and began to pull out goodies for little Albert. "There was a time, Archibald, when you knew my name as well as I know yours."

"Ah, blast and ballast!" swore Archibald. "That's hardly a revelation. Every kid knows about Santa Claus."

"You're right," agreed Santa, with a twinkle in his eye. "Even the boys and girls in your mill towns and coal towns."

"Wa- wa-" Archibald was perturbed. His face went crimson, and his eyes bulged. "Why, if it weren't for me, their fathers wouldn't have jobs!"

"Why don't you sit down, son? I'm concerned about you. You look quite bowled over."

"Santa!" Archibald cried, dropping to his knees and beating his chest in anguish. "Mea culpa! I'm a wicked, wicked man! I'm the worst man in the world!"

"Maybe not," Santa said. "Kaiser Willie has given me no end of trouble, and something tells me he's not done by a long shot. Now, catch your breath and blow your nose. That's it. Maybe ol' Santa has something in his bag for you."

"Is it another bunch of switches?" Archibald asked him, remembering a certain Christmas in his childhood.

Santa made no reply, but went straight to his work. He filled the two stockings, then turned with a flask in his hand. He took a swig and let Archibald have a nip. "Ho, I almost forgot," he said, laughing. He dug into his bag and pulled out a box. He removed the lid to reveal a small candied heart. It was bright red with a hard, sugar coating that reflected the gaslights. And it was beating.

"What in the name of creation is that?" asked Archibald, staring at the thing with fear and revulsion. "The damn thing is alive!"

"It's a heart, son. You wanted a new one, didn't you?"

"Yes, but what am I supposed to do with it?"

"Why swallow it, of course." Santa turned to drain a glass of milk that sat waiting on a Duncan Phyfe table, then hoisted his bag over his shoulder with a grunt. "Well? If you're going to turn your nose up at it, I'll take it back and give it to some other whimpering, self-pitying tyrant."

"No, I want it!" insisted Archibald, and he popped the beating, candied heart into his mouth and swallowed.

"There," Santa said, with a satisfied sigh. "That should give the world a little more peace."

"How long does it take to work, sir?" Archibald asked, meekly.

"Ho! Ho! Ho!" Santa shook with mirth. Then, laying a finger aside his nose, he squeezed himself up the chimney quickly to keep from catching fire. "Merry Christmas, Archibald MacTavish!" he shouted from the rooftop. And then he was gone.

The next morning, Eleanor was twisting her hair into a fashionable construction when she heard a rap at her bedroom door. It was

Mary, her maid. The girl's face was contorted with worry. This was nothing new, for Mary was given to dread. She was particularly spooked by fog, which was unfortunate since she lived in Boston.

"Merry Christmas, Mary."

"Merry Christmas, madam," replied Mary, her eyes darting about like flies at a picnic.

"Is something wrong, dear?"

"I think there's something ailing Mister MacTavish, madam. He ain't—I mean, he isn't himself."

"What do you mean?" Eleanor glanced at the girl's reflection in the mirror. "Is he being contrary?"

"That's just it," said Mary, her chin quivering. "He isn't being mean at all. He's being kind! I think he's come down with fever."

"Really?" asked Eleanor, applying powder to her face. "Let's not be rash in sending for the doctor."

"But madam—"

"Please!" hissed Eleanor, her patience at an end. She slammed down her brush and rose from the dressing table. "Must I be made uneasy before I breakfast?" She closed her eyes, collecting herself. When she opened them again, she smiled and said sweetly, "Come, Mary, let's not fret. It's Christmas, dear."

She patted the maid on the cheek and went downstairs to the breakfast room. Little Albert came running to greet her as she entered. He was cute as a button in his burgundy-velvet suit and Peter Pan collar, and he radiated joy and energy.

"Mommy!" he burst out. "This is the best Christmas ever!"

"Is it, darling? Please don't shout."

"Sorry." Albert lowered his voice to a less strident tone. "I believe Father intends to take me riding in the park, today."

"Riding?" Eleanor was confused. "Do you mean...in Cabot's horseless contraption?" Her husband and sons laughed at her, as though she'd said something terrifically funny. "I'm afraid I don't understand. Do you mean on a horse?"

"I expect t'will be a pony," little Albert replied. "May I go play with my puppets?"

"Yes, dear," said Eleanor, vacantly. "If you've finished your breakfast."

"Hooray!"

Eleanor looked down the length of the table at Archibald, and she was disturbed by what she saw. He was behaving oddly. He smiled at her, even winked at her, and he laughed uproariously. He glowed with the health of a freshly scrubbed schoolboy; his cheeks were flushed; and his eyes were sparkling. He looked so profoundly insipid that it hurt her to see it.

"Archibald," she said, pivoting in her chair to take a serving of sausage from an Irish lad named Tom, "do you really mean to take little Albert riding?"

"I do, my dearest Poopsie!" declared Archibald, causing Cabot to snicker. "I'm going to try that new saddle."

"But only last night, you said you were frightened of horses."

"True," he admitted, "but a man must face his fears, Eleanor. He must fight on to the summit, no matter the odds! Remember that, Cabot!"

"Gee, Pop," said Cabot, "you sound like Roosevelt!"

"Bully!" Archibald cried, slamming the arms of his chair. "That Roosevelt's not such a bad card. I'm beginning to think he's been right about a number of things."

"It's fatigue." Eleanor went to her husband, checked his forehead for fever, and looked into his eyes. "You'd better go upstairs, dear. You're not yourself this morning."

"I'll say he's not!" agreed Cabot, his freckled face stretched by a toothy grin. "Pop has promised to finance my flying machine."

"Oh!" gasped Eleanor. "Poor Archibald!"

"What is wrong with this household?" Archibald asked. "So far as I know, I'm not dead. Cheer up! It's Christmas! Ring the bells! Stuff the bird! Give alms to the poor! My goodness, I could go on and on like that."

And he did go on and on like that. In the following months, it was clear his newfound generosity and kindness were not short-lived. He made concessions to his workers. He cut their hours and increased their pay. He decreased the mark-up at his company stores, and he hired architects to plan better housing. He established college scholarships for his employees' children, and he founded schools in the mill towns and coal towns. He was tireless in his efforts to make the world a better place—even Gertrude Moore was impressed—but not everyone was singing his praises.

"What am I to do?" Eleanor asked, the following July, as she lounged aboard an anchored yacht on Nantucket Sound. "He's obviously gone mad."

She was speaking to Cornelius Rembrandt-the-third, who was the grandson of THE Cornelius Rembrandt, the old lion who'd dominated Northeastern society for the last forty-five years. This youngest Cornelius—or 'Bunny', as he was called—was a handsome fellow with blond hair and a long, patrician nose. He was something of a Beau Brummell, and that day, he was wearing a white, red-striped blazer, a powder-blue bow tie, and a straw boater.

"Archibald may well be mad," conceded Bunny, swirling his scotch in a cut-crystal glass, "but you'll never get him committed. He's too filthy rich, and there are too many people making money off him."

"I'm at my wits end," Eleanor said. "Really, I am. At the rate at which he's giving away money, I shall be lucky to afford new tweeds next season. His antics have cost me socially, as well. I failed to receive an invitation to the Peabody ball."

"You didn't? How dare they!"

"Even the Longyears are avoiding me."

"Those upstarts!" Bunny poured some more scotch into their glasses. "Blood means nothing anymore. People get above themselves."

"Oh, it's so refreshing to hear someone say that aloud. I have to watch my tongue around Saint Archibald, and it seems he's always in Boston now. I think he's put aside his mistress."

"The vixen?" Bunny smiled. "Well...that needn't spoil our fun. You'll find ways of breaking free for a week or two, hm? Listen, mio cara, I've been hearing some rather nasty rumors running through the law circles. Foster Smith-Wilson told me that Archibald was drawing up a new will."

"No!"

"Yes, and there's more." Bunny moved closer to Eleanor and took her hands in his. "The boys will only get a million each, and you'll be left with the Boston house and a measly five-hundred-thousand."

"That's wretched!" she screamed, with uncharacteristic energy. "I'll be a pauper! He can't do it!"

"He can, mio cara, and he will," said Bunny. He pulled her to him and held her close. "Leave him and be mine. We'll travel the world together."

"Don't." She shrugged out of his embrace and tidied her blouse. "You know I can't abide scandal. Besides, I have to think of my boys."

"There's only one alternative," Bunny told her, and then he paused. The yacht creaked as it rocked atop the water. "I think you know what that is, darling."

"You're as mad as he is," she said. "But at least you're more interesting. Go on."

"I have a birthday next month. Wouldn't it be a grand thing if you and Archibald were to join me in Newport?"

"I don't know, Bunny." Eleanor stood and fanned herself with a handkerchief. "Let's go back, shall we? It's hot, and you're making me nervous."

Eleanor and Archibald arrived in Newport in late August, as a tropical depression ricocheted off the New England coast. They were soaked through by the time they stepped into Bunny's cavernous "cottage," and the wind-driven rain continued to beat against the French windows and mansard roof. The floors, walls, and staircases were covered in white marble, which was damp to the touch due to heavy humidity. The place reminded Archibald of a crypt, and he would have joked about it, had not the display of extravagant wealth disgusted him.

"Look at this place," he said to Eleanor.

"I am," she replied, dreamily. "It's Nephelokokkugia."

"Nephel who?"

"Nephelokokkugia, dear. That's Greek for 'cloud-cuckoo-land'."

"It's cuckoo alright," scoffed Archibald. "Downright crazy to spend so much money on a residence. No respectable person builds on this scale today. You know why?"

"Why, dear?"

"Because man has evolved, that's why!"

Bunny was off securing his yacht against the storm, so Eleanor and Archibald were greeted and shown to their rooms by a houseboy—a Portuguese mute, who had the name "Alphonso" pinned to the back of his jacket. Archibald found the lack of servants puzzling. He would have thought that a place that size should be brimming with servants. He tried to question Alphonso about the staff, but the brute simply groaned and scratched his flat head.

As night fell, the storm intensified, and the old mansion rumbled. Bunny returned in time to dress for dinner. He warmly greeted his two guests and apologized for the shortage of servants.

"It's the storm," he explained, as he offered his arm to Eleanor and led the way into the dining room. "I thought it best to send away most of the staff. Let them be responsible for their own safety. There's only Cook and Alphonso left, so I won't promise that dinner will go smoothly. Alphonso has never served at table, and he's not exactly dainty. Handy chap to have around, though."

Dinner was superb. Beluga crepes were served with Dom Perignon, followed by bisque and a Maderia. Poached sole in a dill sauce was accompanied by a pert Sonnenhur and grilled pheasant by a Chateau-Latour. The main course was a leg of lamb, spicy and succulent. After the cheese platter came an airy soufflé and a glass of Chateau d'Yquem. Fruit and nuts were then brought in with coffee and a piece of Belgian chocolate. After the Napoleon brandy was poured, Bunny took Archibald into the billiard room and offered him a cigar.

"No, thank you," declined Archibald. "I gave up cigars last Christmas." Bunny made no reply to this, so Archibald took a look around the room. "You've got this room packed with curiosities, don't you? Every sort of gewgaw, falderal, and knickknack."

"I suppose it is a bit crowded," Bunny admitted. "I've always fancied clutter. It comforts me. Take this harpoon, for example." He reached to remove the projectile from its rack above the mantle. "It's deceptively light, for something so lethal."

"That comforts you?"

"Yes, it does in a way. I take solace in its sleekness, its timeless efficiency. Holding a thing that is well made, I am assured that perfection does exist in the world, and therefore, there is meaning. You understand?"

"Not really," Archibald replied, "but I'm glad I'm not a whale."

"Clever," said Bunny. "Shall we play a game of billiards?"

"I'd rather not, sir, if you don't mind. I've had a bit more than my share of drink tonight, and I'm feeling a tad inebriated. May we sit?"

"By all means, Archibald."

"Don't you think you should put away that harpoon?"

"Oh, yes, how silly of me."

The two men continued conversing. They spoke of the stock exchange and touched on politics. Archibald finished his brandy, and his eyes grew heavy. He dozed, snapped himself awake, and dosed again. His arm fell over the arm of his chair, and his mustache twitched with the vibrations of each snore.

Bunny gingerly stood. He crept across to the mantle and removed the harpoon from the rack. He tiptoed to Archibald's chair and aimed his harpoon for the center of the back of it. Just as he was about to thrust it through, Archibald woke himself with a snore. He mumbled and shook his head. Startled, Bunny lost his balance and faltered. In a desperate attempt to get solid footing, he firmly planted his harpoon... into his own foot. He screamed, pulled it out, and began to hop about the room.

"Are you all right, there, good fellow?" asked Archibald.

"Splendid," Bunny said, through his teeth. "Only a cramp."

"It's no wonder—the two of us nodding off like that. You'll work it off climbing those marble stairs. I'll bid you good night, then."

Archibald retired to his bed, and Bunny sneaked into Eleanor's room. He showed her his "boo-boo" and cried on her shoulder. He bit into the bed hangings as Eleanor poured scotch onto the wound. She bandaged his foot and was kissing him, when there was a knock at her door.

"It's Archibald!" Eleanor whispered.

"What's he doing here?" asked Bunny. "I thought you said he no longer comes to you at night."

"He doesn't. He gave it up last Christmas. Quick, get in the wardrobe!"

Bunny climbed in the wardrobe, and Eleanor hid the bandages, shoe, and stocking. She misted herself and the room with perfume and flattened the wrinkles on the bed. She composed herself and opened the door.

"Poopsie, have you seen my gray morning coat?" Archibald asked her, entering. "You don't suppose your Mary accidentally packed it with your things, do you? Shall I have a look in the wardrobe?"

"No!" shouted Eleanor. "I mean, no, I'm certain she didn't. I had to unpack myself, since there were no servants. I'm certain you've over-looked it. I'll help you search, first thing in the morning. All right, dear?"

"I'm getting old, Eleanor," he said, giving her a chaste kiss on the forehead. "I'm starting to lose things."

"Good night, Archibald."

When he had gone, the door to the wardrobe squeaked open, and Bunny emerged. He kissed Eleanor, told her to be brave, and hopped off down the hall to his rooms. He stretched out on his bed and contemplated his next move.

The wind gradually died, but sporadic lightning continued. When the captain's clock atop his bedroom mantle struck three, Bunny left his rooms and moved through the dark hallway. He reached Archibald's door, deftly turned the knob and entered. He hobbled around the bed, listening acutely to the rise and fall of Archibald's snores. A large target took shape in the shadows. Bunny pulled a revolver from the pocket of his monogrammed robe and stuck a fat pillow over Archibald's face. Then he fired, and goose feathers flew everywhere. He lifted the pillow and, seeing flowing blood, ran back to Eleanor and told her that he had successfully murdered her husband.

"I don't believe it," she said. "What have you done?"

"What have WE done, you mean. You're mine for life, now. I own you and always will. I can do whatever I like with you."

"But if we're caught—"

"We won't be caught." Bunny took her face in his hands and began to kiss it. "Mmm, mio cara!"

"What will you do with the body?"

"Alfonso will take it to the dock. The surf is up from the storm. The waves will slam the body against the rocks. There will be nothing left by the time the sharks are finished. Nothing to discover. He drowned in the storm, and his body was washed out to sea. That's all. Now, kiss me."

Alfonso hated messy clean-up jobs. Perhaps it would have cheered him to know that this would be his last. Before he could roll the body off the dock, Archibald returned to consciousness. They looked at each other and screamed, and a rogue wave slapped them both off the dock and into the turbulent ocean. They struggled to stay afloat, and Alfonso was sucked off to Ireland.

Once again, Archibald escaped assassination. The bullet only grazed the side of his head, and the feathers and blood obscured the insignificant wound. He was knocked out for a while and now had a headache, but his health was otherwise intact. He made his way to the shore and collapsed on the dunes. He coughed up seawater—and with it, the small, candied heart. It dissolved into the sand.

The lust for vengeance suddenly took hold of him. He pulled himself up and staggered back to the mansion. He took the harpoon from the billiard room and climbed the marble staircase. He found Eleanor and Bunny entwined in sleep, so he skewered them. He dragged the bodies to the dock, found an ax in the boathouse, and chopped the lovers into pieces. He fed the steaks to the sharks and the entrails to the seagulls. The next day, he cleaned up the mess and told the police that his beloved wife and his best buddy were swept out to sea.

The following Christmas Eve, Archibald stood before his two sons in the library of his New York brownstone. He took a dollar bill from his pocket and held it to a candle on the tree. He then placed the bill beneath a dozen seasoned logs in the fireplace, and he nursed the flames until they licked halfway up the chimney. Settling back in his chair, he puffed on his cigar and sipped his brandy.

"Pop!" shouted Albert, who was running about dressed in an Apache costume. "That's a big fire!"

"Yes, Albert, it is," agreed Archibald. "We're going to have such a fire, each and every Christmas Eve!"

Chapter 12

OLGA AND
THE MAGIC SHOES

ASTASYA ANDREVNA KARANAVANOFFSKY WAS KNOWN AS Olga to her friends and adoring public. She was a wee beauty with a waspish waist and big, green eyes. At seventeen, she was the most exciting ballerina to come along in years. The citizens of Saint Petersburg adored her. The critics demanded that she be promoted to prima ballerina assoluta, and the directors of the Imperial Majesty Theatres acquiesced, although they thought she had by no means reached the perfection of her form. Still, a promise from Olga was better than perfection from any other dancer in Russia.

She had a special gift. She had an almost mystical ability to communicate with her body and an instinctual grace. She did not reach for an arabesque nor did she evolve into one. She was placed there, as if by Heaven, and she hung there, en pointe, in ecstasy, suspended in time and space. Her pirouettes were not unlike the spinning of caramelized sugar in that the mind could barely register one dazzling rotation before another and yet another was laid upon it.

As much as her premature elevation, it was Olga's talent that disturbed the more established stars of the Imperial Majesty Ballet. They were enraged by the ease with which she executed the most complex sequences, and they felt betrayed by Heaven when they saw her ability far surpassed their own. They never confessed what they knew in their hearts to be true: that they were all second rate compared to Olga. They were too busy discussing the flaws they imagined in her.

"If her ass gets any bigger," complained one ballerina, in the dressing room between acts, "it's going to take a Cossack to pair her lifts."

"If her breasts get any bigger," another ballerina countered, "they'll make her empress of all the Russias."

There was no arguing with success, however, and Olga had that in spades. She was particularly beloved for resurrecting the Tchaikovsky ballets, which had fallen out of fashion. People now came from as far away as London and Paris to see her dance the role of Aurora. The Prince of Wales called her "Heaven's Marionette," and the French ambassador described her as an "enfante cherie." It was even said that the Czarina paid some monks to constantly pray for the good health and long dance life of Olga.

With such unparalleled success came the inevitable barrage of suitors. Flowers, telegrams, and jewelry crowded her dressing room nightly. She could not exit the theatre by any door without a flock of male admirers begging a word or autograph, and her maid Varya was forever turning men away from Olga's house.

Her most persistent suitor was Prince Ilya Vladimirovich Rulykin. A widower at thirty-two, Prince Rulykin was a handsome rogue. He was tall and aristocratic, and he wore his hair pomaded and swept back from his high brow. His fleshy lips suggested salacity, and—in this, at least—his lips did not lie. He was fanatically pursuing carnal pleasure when he stumbled into a performance of 'Sleeping Beauty'. He took one look at Olga and was enchanted, and thereafter, fanatically pursued her. He took a box and was found there at her every performance. He sent her roses six days a week, and fabulous pieces of jewelry, which were returned to him. He connived to see her alone, using the tried-and-true tactics of his lecherous past, but Olga would not receive him. He composed a heart-wrenching letter of proposal, but this, too, was returned unopened. His sleep grew fitful, his nights on the town lost their appeal, and his temper grew foul.

"Did Your Highness enjoy last evening?" his valet Sasha asked him, one morning. "Was Olga in good form?"

"Shut up, you lout!" shouted Prince Rulykin. "How dare you speak her name with familiarity. You are nothing, while she is a gift to Mother Russia! And how many times must I tell you not to speak when you shave me?"

His mood did not improve at breakfast. From the moment he entered his mother's "Lapis-lazuli Room," he was churlish and fidgety. Deep, peevish sighs steamed from the hot springs of his discomfort, and he hid his anguished face behind the pages of a conservative newspaper. His mother made two attempts at small talk before becoming incensed.

"This is too much, Ilya Vladimirovich!" she exclaimed, slapping her napkin against the edge of the table. Her pearl drop earrings swung in irregular arcs as her head trembled. "Will you make no attempt to amuse me? If you want to be dreary, go to Moscow!" She retrieved a hand mirror that was attached by a ribbon to her gray, silk robe and examined her snow-white coiffure. "This is about your ridiculous attachment to that ballerina, isn't it? She's had the good sense to refuse you."

"She has not refused me!" insisted the Prince.

"Nyet?" His mother lifted her painted-on eyebrows, squinted her eyes, and pursed her lips. She looked like some ghastly geisha who was tittering at the sight of a man's naked body. She kept the expression plastered on her face as she crossed the room and draped herself across a fainting couch. "She will refuse you, you know. A girl like that doesn't marry. I've known a few ballerinas. They don't need men. A man could never give them the pleasure that dance does. Your rival is Dance, Ilya Vladimirovich, and he's a better lover than you."

"What kind of mother are you?" he asked, and spat on the floor. "I curse you! How can you take delight in your own son's misery? Go to the devil!"

She laughed at him. He threw a vase against the wall, but she only laughed harder. He kicked over his chair and stormed from the room. His mother's cruel laughter followed him down the hall, echoing off the marble. He covered his ears and ran, screaming.

Late the next morning, a fine carriage with a coat of arms painted on its doors pulled up in front of Olga's house. Prince Rulykin descended from it with a package in one hand and a pistol in the other. He pushed his way past the footman on the porch and entered the residence. The maid Varya came running to halt his advance. The prince placed the pistol to his temple and swore that he would kill himself unless Olga agreed to accept and wear the gift contained in the package. Varya hurriedly took the package upstairs to Olga, who, after a moment's hesitation, tore off the bow and paper and opened the box.

"Why, Miss!" cried Varya, peering over her lady's shoulder. "It's a pair of pointe shoes!"

The shoes were dainty and exquisitely crafted. The soles were wafer-thin and made of high-grade, durable leather. The stitching was close, and the pink satin had been embroidered with tiny snowflakes. There were small bows attached to the back of each shoe. They were meant to be wings for Olga's heels, and they were the same pastel green as her eyes.

"What am I to do with such a man, Varya?" she asked. "What if he proposes marriage in a similar fashion?"

"They're only shoes, Miss," Varya told her. "He didn't send a ring."

"I suppose I could wear them to a rehearsal." Olga put the shoes back in the box. "Go down and tell him that I will wear the shoes but once. And tell him to leave me alone!"

Prince Rulykin rejoiced when Varya gave him Olga's message, and he even gave the footman a ruble. There was no doubt in the prince's mind that he would bed the ballerina. Assured of his ultimate victory, he allowed his mind to move on to less lofty goals. He decided to go in search of vodka, balalaikas, and chubby harlots. Climbing back into his carriage, he ordered his coachmen to drive to a tavern on the outskirts of Saint Petersburg.

Olga's life was forever changed by those pointe shoes, for when she put them on and danced, euphoria engulfed her. She felt supremely confident, and she literally could not put a foot wrong. The first night she performed in them, the audience was stupefied. They sat silent for several moments before roaring their appreciation. The critics heaped praise upon her. Even Jacque Maurite—the old, frail, ballet master who was notoriously stingy with compliments—fell to her feet and kissed them.

"I must get my hands on more of those shoes," Olga said to Varya, a few nights later. Varya was brushing Olga's hair, which was dark red and billowy. Olga pushed a strand of it back from her face and narrowed her eyes. "I know what I must do, Varya. I will agree to marry Prince Rulykin if he promises me a lifetime supply of those shoes. What do you think?"

"Well, Miss..." Varya was reticent.

"What?" pressed Olga. "If you've got something to say, say it, you goose."

"Why must you marry a man you do not love, Miss? It is the shoes you want, not the prince. Why don't you find out who owns the company that makes those shoes? Who knows? Maybe the owner is a handsome industrialist of honorable character. You could marry him, instead, and be assured of an endless supply of shoes."

The next afternoon, Olga put on her best tea gown and received Prince Rulykin in her salon. She smiled at him, prettily, and allowed him to kiss her three times, 'a la Russe. She poured him a brandy, clipped and lit his cigar, and giggled at his jokes. When she had lulled him into a state of comfort, she casually inquired about the company that manufactured the shoes.

"Company?" The prince took offense. "There is no company. Do you think those shoes could be mass-produced, daragaja? How silly you are! They were made by a cobbler. I understand he lives in the woods outside Tavda."

"Where is Tavda?" Olga asked him. "Is it near Saint Petersburg?"

"Nyet," said Prince Rulykin, with a chuckle. "Tavda is far away from here. East of the middle-Urals. You wouldn't want to go there. Come closer, and let me admire that swan neck of yours."

"That is that," Olga told Varya, in the dressing room, that evening. "I shall have to marry the prince now. I can hardly marry a poor cobbler."

"But he may be a good-looking cobbler, Miss! What if he is as strong as a bear and as wise as an owl?"

"A wise peasant?" Olga threw back her head and laughed. "I am Olga! I cannot marry a muzhik."

"To marry the prince is to marry beneath you," insisted Varya. "He will never be true to you. He is not that sort of man. They say he is immoral—that he is fond of absinthe and orgies."

"I have heard these rumors," Olga confessed. "Well, he may have his pleasures—what of it? I will have my shoes."

"Please listen, Miss!" Varya stopped fussing with Olga's tutu and stood to look her lady in the eye. "The maker of those shoes is surely a remarkable man. He has a gift from Heaven. That gives you something in common. It would be better to marry a peasant favored by the angels than to marry a prince doomed to damnation."

"This is nonsense!" protested Olga. "I don't want to marry a cobbler, and I'm certainly not going to live in some remote forest. For whom would I dance, hm? For the wolves? I tell you I shall never go to Tavda!"

A week later, Olga suffered a severe setback when Prince Rulykin's body was fished out of the Moika Canal. He had shot himself on the quay and fallen into the water. Word soon got about that he'd been scorned by the prima donna of the Imperial Opera, who told him she loved her music more than men. This meant that Olga's supply of magical pointe shoes was cut off abruptly.

As the months went by, the shoes in her possession began to disintegrate before her horrified eyes. The little snowflakes became shabby tufts of dirty, unraveled silk. The material on the toes wore off altogether, and had to be patched. The pastel-green bows grew soiled and then vanished, leaving holes. The critics wrote that Olga was cheap and that her shoes were a disgrace to Russian ballet. Her dancing began to suffer, and attendance at her performances dropped considerably. She despaired and begged for a leave of absence. Upon gaining it, she packed a trunk for a journey east.

Olga and Varya went by train from Saint Petersburg to Vologda. They took a troika to Kirov and a carriage across the middle-Ural Mountains to Sosva. There, they boarded a ferry that took them down the Sosva and Tavda Rivers. They reached the town of Tavda just before Lent, and took a room above an unsanitary tavern. Exhausted, they collapsed onto flea-ridden, straw mattresses and fell asleep.

The next morning, they set out to locate the cobbler. It did not take them long because everyone they spoke to knew of Mendel, the irascible cobbler. He lived alone in a cabin, some distance from town. Olga hired a stooped blacksmith to serve as guide, and he led the two women into the white-birch forest. They walked for nearly an hour before reaching a log cabin. It was small and dilapidated. There were shingles missing from its roof, and the porch steps were rotten. The one window had a broken pane, into which a man's undergarment had been stuffed. More articles of clothing were hung out to dry on rusty nails and tree limbs. Olga and Varya were dismayed by the unkempt place and shocked at the sight of the cobbler.

Mendel was attractive, as Varya had predicted, and was probably wise, judging from his wide brow and wary eyes. Although he was short, his shoulders were broad, and his muscles clung to his damp, peasant shirt. His hair was black, and his eyebrows were thick. He was olive-skinned and a bit bowlegged. He had a big nose, and his nostrils flared fiercely. Perhaps he was not handsome in the classic or courtly sense, but Olga was mesmerized by his magnetism. Unfortunately, he found nothing compelling in her.

"What do you want?" he yelled, as he charged at them with a shovel. "Go away! You're not wanted!"

"Not wanted?" repeated Olga, forlornly.

"Go away!"

"Be still and listen, you fool!" Varya shouted, stomping her foot. "This lady is the greatest ballerina in the world! Do you understand? All the aristocrats in Saint Petersburg throw themselves at her feet, but she has come to throw herself at yours! Are you not grateful?"

"I don't want any ballerina throwing herself at me," Mendel told her. "I don't want any woman. I don't need anybody. I want to be alone. Go away!"

"I don't understand," said Olga. "How can a miserable misanthrope like you make such magical shoes?"

"Don't call me names, you stupid slut. What do you know about my shoes, anyway?"

"She knows a great deal about your magical shoes," Varya assured him, then she turned to wipe away Olga's tears and embrace her.

"I don't believe in magic." Mendel sneered, and his nostrils twitched derisively. "But if there is magic in your shoes, it certainly wasn't me who put it there. I'm a cobbler, not a warlock. Go away!"

"The shoes are magical," insisted Olga. "I know they are. They must be."

"Begging your pardon, Miss," the stooped blacksmith said, nudging Olga with his elbow. "It might be Brother Dmitri that puts the magic in your shoes."

"Who?" asked the women.

"Brother Dmitri Dmitrivich Dmitrianko, Misses. He's a holy monk."

"Holy, my ass!" ejaculated Mendel. "He's a fraud!"

"He's a holy starets," the blacksmith asserted. "When the men from town pick up the ballet shoes from Mendel, they take them to Brother Dmitri for a blessing. He, in turn, sends them to our mayor, who sends them off to Saint Petersburg. It all works rather nicely."

"Where may I find Brother Dmitri?" Olga inquired. "Is he in a local monastery?"

"Hah!" Mendel planted his shovel into the earth, and folded his arms. "In a local whorehouse, more likely!"

But Brother Dmitri had no need of brothels, as Olga found out that evening when she went, alone, to his house. She knocked and knocked at the door until she finally opened it and entered. She was alarmed to hear rumbles and crashes coming from the room above her, and her eyebrows soared when she heard squeals of gaiety.

She climbed to the top of a creaky staircase and discovered five naked women, who were leaping about like fawns in a forest glade. They were being chased by a bear of a man, and he wasn't wearing a stitch of clothes either. One of the women saw Olga and pointed. Her companions paused, then burst into hysterical laughter. The man laughed so hard that he fell to all fours and pounded the floor with the palm of his hand.

He was a large man in every way, and he was hairy, too. His salt-and-pepper beard hung down to his knees, and it was weighted with particles of food. The hair on his head was also long and matted, and his mustache was dripping with substance. His stomach jiggled with loose fat, but his limbs were taut with muscle. When he rose from the floor, he towered above the women.

His height was awesome, but his eyes were more remarkable. They were so large they seemed to pop out of his head. The whites of them were bloodshot and glassy, presumably from too much vodka. His irises were an odd milky gray, and his pupils twinkled. They were piercing eyes. Olga thought them hypnotic eyes, as they glared at her.

"Who are you, woman?" the man bellowed, in a deep bass.

"I am Nastasya Andrevna Karanavanoffsky, from Saint Petersburg," she answered. She wanted to look away or run, but his eyes held her fast. "Please, call me Olga."

"I'll call you whatever I want," said he.

"Are you Brother Dmitri Dmitrivich Dmitrianko?"

"I am."

"Then I must speak with you."

The monk commanded his bare ladies to leave, and they did so with shrieks of disappointment. Brother Dmitri put on a pilgrim's robe and sat Olga down at a table. He poured her some tea from a samovar, took her tiny hands in his, and began to suck on her fingertips.

"Oh—I—please—" stammered Olga. "I—please—PLEASE!"

"You have come about the pointe shoes, haven't you?" he asked her, as he paused between her thumb and index finger.

"But how did you know? That's miraculous! You must be the holiest man in all Russia! That is truly the most—oh—I—please—I—PLEASE!"

"You like?" He paused again and smiled, knowingly. "You like."

"We mustn't," she half-heartedly protested. "It would be a sin."

"Don't think of it as sin," he told her, his wild eyes coming closer to hers. "Think of it as a prerequisite of redemption. Come, touch me. Smell me!"

"But the magic shoes—"

"We talk of shoes, later."

They did speak of shoes, when Brother Dmitri was throwing Olga out the next morning. She did not go quietly. She wrapped her arms and legs around his bare torso and held on for dear life. He pried her off, pinned her to the wall, and tried to reason with her.

"Little Olga," he said, sternly, "you must go back to Saint Petersburg. I have no further need of you. Everything is fluid and mutatable, and this is especially true of passion. Repent the sin you have committed here and return to the calling you were given. Go dance, little Olga."

"I'm not leaving this burg without those shoes!" Olga sobbed. "I want my magic shoes!"

"There is no magic in those shoes."

"There must be!"

"There is not," insisted Brother Dmitri. "Da, I give shoes my blessing, but nichevo! I have also given my blessing to people who died the next day. The magic in those shoes is the magic in you. It is the magic that Heaven has placed within you. So, go and give your magic to the world and get out of my house!"

Olga's return to the Saint Petersburg stage was a resounding triumph. The critics agreed she had never danced so divinely. She went on to dance for many years, until the Bolshevik Revolution. She then grabbed her jewels and fled to Buenos Aires. There, she met a dashing gigolo named Rico. Dazzled by Olga's glamour, he abandoned his profession and married her. She bore him twin sons, both of whom took up the tango.

Chapter 13

CECIL AND THE YOGI

HERE ONCE LIVED A WISE MAHARANI PRAISED FOR HER grace and beauty, though she'd seen eighty years come and go. Her palaces and subjects were in Northern India, but Princess Santha—as she was called by the British—long made it her habit to roam about the subcontinent, according to the fashionable seasons. Because of its cosmopolitan society, she preferred Bombay to any other spot. When in town, she took a penthouse suite atop the Wellington Hotel, and the higher castes, both Hindu and Christian, came to pay homage to her charm.

On Sundays, while the good British prayed in their temples, and the bad British nursed their hangovers, Princess Santha seized the opportunity to rest. The Hindus in her entourage were told to seek their entertainment elsewhere, and most of her servants she turned loose upon the city. Only two guests were received into her Sunday inner sanctum, and both of them were men.

Hari Kamalakar habitually arrived at noon. In his day, Hari was a celebrated master of Sanskrit chant, but he was now over seventy and vowed nevermore to sing. He often reminisced about his glory days, yet he was not chained to his past. He enjoyed life, and life enjoyed him. If he occasionally displayed snobbery, he made up for it by being jolly. Arriving at the Wellington with a bouquet of lilies, he greeted the Maharani and kissed her hand. They then sat down to gossip about their fellow Brahmans.

Around one o'clock, Lord Cecil Pennington-West would arrive with a bottle of gin tucked under his arm. An affable young man, and a cousin to the viceroy, Lord Cecil was handsome in that raised-eyebrow, overbite, English way. Upon his arrival, the conversation would switch to gossip of the Raj.

The three friends competed to talk and amuse until one forty-five, when they sat down to a simple lunch. The menu never varied—vegetable curry and oil pickles—but at least it was filling. A game of cards usually followed, which the maharani always won. She would scoop up her earnings and shriek with laughter, as the smoke from her Russian cigarettes arched over her head like the fiery ring of Shiva.

One Sunday, Princess Santha was concerned to find Lord Cecil in a gloomy mood. She did not approve of brooding, and she thought the English too prone to it. She said many times to her Hindu friends that the English seemed always to be wishing for something that could not possibly be granted. She sometimes lost patience with them, and she did so with Lord Cecil that afternoon, as they sat at lunch.

"What are these sighs you are breathing?" she asked him. "It is my thinking that you are bored with Hari and me."

"Not at all, Princess," Lord Cecil assured her.

"Then, what is it?" She stared at him intently. "Perhaps you need an adventure."

"That's it!" Hari said, for he was a big believer in adventures. "The young fellow needs distraction."

"Ahhh," sighed Lord Cecil. "I thought, at first, I might be taking on malaria, but Doctor Vaughan said not. He couldn't find anything wrong with me. The visit was quite tedious. Well, you know how the Welsh can be."

"Maybe this malaise is not of the body, 'ol chap," suggested Hari. "Maybe you are ill in spirit."

"Yes, I thought of that," Lord Cecil confessed. "I tried to make an appointment with the bishop, but he's off playing cricket in

Mangalore."

"Oh, ho!" cried Hari, his belly shaking beneath his silk tunic. "You English are most peculiar. Why not try one of our holy men, if yours are otherwise engaged?"

"Well..." Lord Cecil was torn between politeness and horror. "Well...you see..."

"Listen, 'ol chap, I know of a brahmana in Uttar Pradesh who is said to be the reincarnation of a wise mahatma. It is the fashion now to visit him, but he is not easy to reach. He lives in a cave at the foot of the Himalaya, and there are bandits who attack the pilgrims. You would need guides."

"But this is the hand of fate!" Princess Santha exclaimed, waving her hands with excitement. "Only yesterday, I received a letter from my grand-nephew, the Raja Rashmi, and he is planning a pilgrimage to this holy man they call Yogi Basu. If I know young Rashmi, he will be taking along servants and luxurious provisions. Shall I send you to his palace in Bihar with a letter of introduction? Why not, eh? That way, you will travel to this yogi in high style."

"Excellent idea!" declared Hari, clapping his hands. "What do you think, 'ol chap? Do you dare go?"

"Why not?" Lord Cecil replied, pouring himself a hefty gin. "There's nothing laid on at the club."

After an exhausting rail journey across the vast interior of India, Lord Cecil reached Patna. The city sat on the bank of the Ganges in the Northeastern state of Bihar. Although it was night when he got there, the streets were still crowded with merchants and beggars. He found a hotel and paid an exhorbitant sum for a rat-infested room that reeked of curry. Early the next morning, he looked over Princess Santha's directions and set off on a bicycle for Raja Rashmi's estate.

The palace lay three miles outside the city. It was an opulent, seventeenth-century confection, with marble walls, onion domes, and stone latticework. The mixture of tantric carvings and Islamic arches suggested that the palace had endured a turbulent history. Lord Cecil was met at the gate by armed guards and taken to the Raja's reception room.

The Raja's beauty was arresting. He was not a tall man, and his physique was slender; yet he carried himself with majesty. His smooth skin, rubbed with scented oil, was cinnamon-hued; his nose was aquiline, but narrow; and his round, expressive eyes were so dark they appeared to be black. He was dressed in yellow, silk pajamas, and his slim feet were encased in golden slippers. A diamond gleamed from one of his nostrils; strands of pearls dripped from his long neck; and a myriad of jewels adorned his fingers, wrists, and ankles.

"You are most welcome, Lord Pennington-West," he said, refolding his great-aunt's letter of introduction and handing it to an aide. "I shall be glad to have company on my pilgrimage."

"Thank you, Your Highness." Lord Cecil pressed his palms together and bowed from the waist. "When do we leave for Uttar Pradesh?"

"Are you in a hurry, Lord Pennington-West?"

"No, Your Highness. Not especially."

"Good!" Raja Rashmi gestured for his guest to take a seat. "We will remain at my palace for a week or so. You see, we must soon embark on a fast to cleanse our souls, so let us feast while we may. Besides, I want to get to know you. It is a funny thing, but I am certain we have much in common."

"I do not doubt it, Your Highness."

"You must call me Rashmi," insisted the Raja, putting his hand on Lord Cecil's shoulder, "and I will call you Cecil."

Raja Rashmi was an extremely rich man, and he lived an extravagant lifestyle. His officials scoured the globe for anything or anyone that might delight him, and he sampled a little of all they presented. He swam in pleasure from the moment he awoke until the moment he closed his eyes in sleep, and so did Lord Cecil, while he remained at the palace. But the time for feasting ended, and the fasting began.

On the morning of their departure for Uttar Pradesh, a new spectacle presented itself: the Raja's caravan. Fourteen elephants, each fantastically painted and costumed, were to carry the Raja, Lord Cecil, nine riflemen, and a supply of provisions. Twenty-four Sudras, six elite guards, and two professional assassins were to accompany on foot. Lord Cecil climbed up into the royal dais, and his empty stomach turned when the elephant rose and began to plod down the path.

"Rashmi," he said, holding on for dear life, "wouldn't it be prudent to greet this holy man with a muted display of wealth?"

"That would be foolish," replied the Raja, "as the yogi may command us to surrender all our worldly goods. Let us enjoy our trifles while we have them."

"'Surrender all our worldly goods?'" Lord Cecil shuddered.

It was an arduous pilgrimage. The caravan snaked its way into Uttar Pradesh, hugging the border of Nepal. As the terrain grew steeper, the temperature dropped. Lord Cecil wrapped himself in blankets, but his teeth chattered, just the same. His muscles ached and cramped, and he was hungrier than he'd ever been in his life. His mind dwelt on juicy roasts and Yorkshire pudding. He desperately wanted to get this odyssey behind him, yet when they reached the holy man's cave, he was struck with fear.

'What on earth am I doing?' he thought. 'I'm not even a believer in this pagan nonsense. I can't possibly go through with it.'

"All right there, good fellow?" Raja Rashmi asked him. "I say, you're looking a bit pale."

"Me?" Lord Cecil forced a machine gun laugh. "No, I'm in fine form! Never better! Um, after you, Rashmi."

Inside the cave, oil lamps and tapers illuminated statues of various Hindu deities. The smell of musty earth was not completely masked by the clouds of sweet incense, nor was the cold successfully routed by a half-dozen braziers. Several priests moved about in the shadows. They shielded their eyes from the profane appearance of the two pilgrims and scurried off, as though fleeing contagion.

The yogi sat in a lotus position on a mat strewn with flower petals. He chanted a mantra so speedily that his lips had no time to moisten, and white paste formed in the corners of his mouth. He was a skinny man—the word 'emaciated' sprang to Lord Cecil's mind—and his cheeks were sunken. His bald head glistened with perspiration, and his face beamed with bliss. He was attended by three priests, who bade the two pilgrims remove their shoes and kneel. When the yogi ran out of steam with his mantra, he opened his eyes, accepted a gourd of water, and addressed the Raja Rashmi and Lord Cecil.

"I am the yogi Basu," he said in English. "You are to be commended for your wisdom in coming. But now that you are here, you must forget who you are and what has brought you here, for I put it to you that you do not know who you are or why you have come. Go and purify your mind and body with ablutions and more fasting, then return to me. That is all."

"Cheeky fellow," Lord Cecil commented to the Raja, on the way back to their camp. "Look here, when he said fasting, he didn't really mean FASTING, did he? I mean, in England we have hot-cross buns during Lent. Don't you fellows have something like that?"

"My friend," said Raja Rashmi, putting his arm around Lord Cecil's waist, "prepare to suffer."

At the end of five days and six nights with nothing but water, the men returned to the yogi. Their self-denial had sprouted disharmony between them. They had grown quarrelsome and sarcastic, and had said hurtful things to each other. They therefore had much bitterness in their hearts when they knelt on the cave floor.

"I perceive you bring much joy with you," Yogi Basu told them. Then he giggled so crazily that his attendants had to wipe the tears from his eyes. When he recovered himself, he said, "Before each of you has been placed a lamp. Every morning, as I speak to you the words of the day, you will gaze at your lamps and ponder my meaning. Let us begin."

He clapped his hands, and two priests brought him a sandal-wood box. From it, he withdrew a ceremonial mask that had the features of a tiger. He donned it, and as a gong sounded, he stood and spread his arms wide.

"There is a tiger named Violence," he shouted, "and he is feasting on the flesh of peace-loving people!"

Lord Cecil kept an eyebrow raised, expecting some elaboration. When none was forthcoming, and the yogi returned to his lotus position, Lord Cecil prickled with resentment. He huffed and his mind raced.

'A tiger named Violence,' he thought. 'What utter claptrap! Do you mean to say that I've come all this way—to the brink of starvation—so this old fool can parade about in masks and parody Aesop? Does he honestly expect me to kneel here on this damp earth and ponder all day?'

Yet, that is exactly what Lord Cecil did. Whether from boredom or some triumph of the spirit within him, he concentrated on the lamp's flame and on the flesh-eating tiger. The hours dragged, and he was occasionally snapped back to frustration; but to his credit, he stubbornly returned to his objective again and again. The flame. The tiger. The flame. The tiger. The flame and the tiger.

Sometime in the middle of the afternoon, his legs numb and his stomach churning, Lord Cecil entered into what some would call an altered state of consciousness. It might have been induced by his fasting and fatigue, or perhaps he became so narrowly transfixed on the flame that his peripheral vision dissipated, thereby triggering disorientation and hallucination. Or maybe—just maybe—some supernatural hand played a role in his disturbing experience. Whatever the truth, the fact remains that he believed himself to be in the presence of a tiger.

He never saw it but felt its menacing power. He heard its breath and growl. He smelled its damp coat and pungent spray, and he thought he could hear it sharpening its claws against the wall of the cave.

Just as he decided to make a quick exit, a series of images began to flash through his mind like photographs. He saw scenes of war with mangled bodies, severed limbs, and streams of blood. He saw whole towns demolished, burned, and depopulated. He witnessed murder, rape, and all manner of physical and emotional violence. He was never afterward able to convey the full scope of the carnage he encountered in the cave that afternoon, but it clearly left him shaken.

"We endured terror today, my friend," said Raja Rashmi, as they shared a humble meal of paan in their tent that evening. "This means we are strong."

"I'm not going back tomorrow," Lord Cecil told him.

"Will you not?" asked the Raja. "Ah, that is a pity. You were giving me new-found respect for the British."

But Lord Cecil did go back the next morning and the next two mornings after that. Despite his hunger, doubts, and fears, he resolved to see the experience to its end. Each day, Yogi Basu had a new mask and a new meditation:

"There is a cobra named Arrogance, and he is spitting into the eyes of the sacred!"

"There is a scorpion named Greed, and he is stinging the heels of the contented!"

"There is a worm named Indifference, and he is eating the belly of the compassionate!"

Each meditation brought a corresponding set of images to Lord

Cecil's imagination, and each he found uniquely horrifying. The successive days of spiritual torture drained him. He found no rest at night, for the agonizing visions of the day reappeared grotesquely distorted in his nightmares. He told Raja Rashmi that he felt as though he were disappearing and he wasn't sure he gave a damn.

The Raja was in a similar state. His self–importance and physical vanity were stripped, and his fluid grace was shattered. He had become gentle in spirit, and he was quick to show gratitude for every kindness shown him.

"My dear," he said to Lord Cecil, as they climbed to the cave that fifth and last morning, "it is not an exaggeration to say that together, we have borne all injustices throughout the history of the world."

"Let us hope, Rashmi, that we survive what awaits us today."

"I expect we will," the Raja answered, grinning. "Otherwise, who will tell of the yogi's great wisdom?"

They entered the cave and took their places before Yogi Basu. When the master had finished his chanting, he clapped his hands. But this time, instead of a sandalwood box, the priests brought an ivory one; and instead of a mask, the yogi withdrew a headdress made of white feathers. The priests placed it on his head, and he stood to give his meditation.

"There is a dove named Love," he said, softly. "Open the cage of your heart and set her free."

Lord Cecil, no longer a virgin to the process, relaxed his body and focused his mind. The lamp. The dove. The lamp. The dove. The lamp and the dove.

Suddenly a surge of energy coursed through him, and he was filled with a sense of security. The purest images began to flash before him. He saw an infant asleep in its mother's arms, and a cat stretched out on its back in the sun. He was fascinated to see two strangers meet and become instant friends, and he wept to see a poor man's table spread with food. He witnessed ceasefires and the signing of peace treaties, and he saw enemies embrace on the battleground.

Most of all, he saw lovers: kissing in a Montmartre café, snuggling on the banks of the Ganges, making passionate love in the tall grasses of Kenya, splashing about in the Tongan surf, and shopping for engagement rings in Wahoo, Nebraska. The world seemed a virtual Eden—a sphere spinning with endless delight. Never had Lord Cecil known such sublimity or felt such peace of mind.

When he returned to himself, he found the cave transformed. Torches blazed and sitars played, and Yogi Basu was standing on his head. The priests passed around pitchers of coconut milk and platters of roots and masala. The two pilgrims ate their fill and humbly accepted flowered garlands around their necks. They hugged each other; they hugged all of the priests; and they even hugged Yogi Basu.

"I am a new man!" Lord Cecil shouted to Raja Rashmi, as they whirled about dancing. "I see everything so clearly! I will never be the same!"

Two years later, Princess Santha and Hari Kamalakar sat finishing their Sunday lunch of vegetable curry and oil pickles. Age had taken its toll on both of them, but they retained their elegance and wit. When their plates were removed, they left the table and began a game of cards.

"I received a letter last week from Lord Cecil," the Maharani said, in Hindi, as she flicked the ash of her cigarette into an empty teacup.

"Oh?" asked Hari, somewhat frostily. "And is he still on that damp island with that holy man?"

"Yes, he's still in England with the bishop. He writes that he's coming to visit Rashmi in September, and he wonders if we might join them for a month or two. Shall we go up to Bihar? What do you think?"

"I think we should wait and see if we are still living in September," Hari told her. "I do not understand why the English want to linger in England. What is there that can be so captivating?"

"I don't know, Hari." Princess Santha inhaled on her cigarette and shrugged. "Perhaps it's the cricket."

Chapter 14

EZEKIEL AND THE ALIENS

ZEKIEL WAS A FUGITIVE FROM JUSTICE. HE WAS NOT RUNNING from the law, but from a woman. Not just any woman, but Big Lizzie, who was six-feet-seven and weighed in at a whopping three-sixty. She was a prison guard for a Missouri women's institution, and she could kill a man with a single punch.

The trouble began like this. One day, Big Lizzie came down with the sniffles. She returned home early and found Ezekiel atop her room-mate Katrina. Upon being discovered, Katrina started to shriek. Big Lizzie grabbed her by the skinny neck and shook her like a rag mop. While the women were thus occupied, Ezekiel collected his trousers and trumpet and slunk down the fire escape.

Big Lizzie was not the forgiving kind, and her nose could smell a man from as far away as two city blocks. Ezekiel decided to take no chances. He hopped a northbound freight train and left the state of Missouri.

For a while, he shined shoes and slung hash in Peoria. Then he worked in a Chicago armaments factory. After the war, the factory closed, and Ezekiel found himself without a job. He went up to Milwaukee, because he had two cousins who worked there in a brewery. His cousins welcomed him gladly, and let him sleep on their sofa, but they refused to help him get a job at their plant. They said he was too fine of a musician to waste his days bottling beer, and they convinced him to pound the pavement with his horn.

But it was still the Big-Band Era, and trumpet players were a dime a dozen. Ezekiel contented himself with short-lived engagements in mobster-run, gaming dens until he landed a first-chair spot in a band that played Polish weddings. He didn't care much for polkas, but the money was easy, and it sure beat shining shoes. He soon saved enough to get a small apartment, and he bought himself a couple of suits. Things were going well, but then word reached him that a large woman was asking around about him.

"How large?" he asked his landlord.

"About as large as women get," the landlord assured him. "You could fill her shoes with coal and float them down the Milwaukee River."

That was all Ezekiel needed to hear. Concluding that Big Lizzie was hot on his trail, he bid good-bye to his cousins and hopped another train. It was a cold day, and the open car offered no protection from the wind. Ezekiel dug deep in the coal in an attempt to stay warm, but he eventually found he could stand it no longer. When the train was just west of Waukesha, he threw his trumpet case over the side and jumped off after it. He hit the hard earth with a grunt and rolled into a frozen ditch. He climbed out, fetched his trumpet, and limped down a country lane.

He'd gone a half-mile or so when he came to a thicket. As he passed it, a pebble came out of nowhere and hit him in the shoulder. He reached to rub the spot, and another pebble struck him in the buttocks. In the midst of his pain, he looked around and realized that someone was hiding in the shrubs with a slingshot. He roared and charged the thicket, and a white boy took off running. Ezekiel chased him, tackled him, and pinned him to the ground.

"Don't kill me!" the boy pleaded. "I didn't mean no harm!"

He was only about fourteen, and thin as a beanpole. His hair was dirty blond, his face was freckled, and his nose was running with snot. His jug ears were red from the cold, and his buckteeth were chattering. He didn't look like he had a lick of sense, but he didn't look like he had much meanness in him either.

"Stop your screaming, farm boy," Ezekiel told him. "Ain't nobody gonna kill you. If I was gonna kill you, I would've done it by now. Besides, you're the one who was aiming to kill."

"No, I wasn't," blubbered the boy. "I was just having some fun."

"Well, it wasn't fun for me," Ezekiel said, standing to let him up. "S'at what you do with your time, huh? You hide in them bushes and wait for some Negro to come along?"

"Heck, no! There ain't that many Coloreds around here."

"I guess you got lucky today then."

"No! What I mean is...I didn't even think about you being...I ain't never done this before—honest!"

"Uh-huh." Ezekiel handed the boy the slingshot. "I reckon I'll let you have this back, seeing as how you're contrite. You promise to let me pass on through without giving me any more trouble?"

"I promise, Mister," the boy squeaked. "I swear it on my granny's grave."

"You ain't gotta swear. You leave your poor granny to rest in peace." Ezekiel turned to find his trumpet case, and the boy followed him. "You got a name?"

"Yessir, my name's Eddie Schneider. You got one?"

"I'm Ezekiel Jones."

"Ezekiel, eh? Like is in the Bible?"

"That's right, son. Like is in the Bible." Ezekiel retrieved his case and wiped it off with his coat sleeve. "This land belongs to your daddy?"

"No, Pa died in the war." Eddie hung his head and kicked at the earth with the toe of his boot. "He was shot down over Romania."

"I'm sorry."

"Don't be sorry. Pa wanted to be a hero. He hated them Nazis. Ma runs the farm now."

"A dairy farm?"

"That's right."

"She don't need no hands, does she?"

"Aw, Ma can't afford no hands," Eddie told him. "We're barely scraping by as it is, eh?"

"Why don't we go see her anyhow?" suggested Ezekiel. "I need a hot meal and a bed, and I'm a mighty hard worker. Maybe she'll take me on for a night or two."

So Eddie took Ezekiel home. The sun was dipping below the horizon by the time they got there. The farm consisted of a barn, silo, and dairy shed, a small, Gothic-Revival house, and a few acres of rolling pasture. Ezekiel's eyes watered from the pungent stink of manure, and they strained in the dimming light to locate the piles.

Eddie's mother came out on the porch to meet them. She was still young and might have been pretty, had she bothered to spruce up a bit. She wore a brown housedress and a moth-eaten coat, and her hair was pulled back in a tight bun. Her shoes were the kind favored by schoolmarms, and her heavy stockings were rolled halfway down her legs. There was nothing pleasing in the way she moved. When she spoke, her tone made it clear that she would tolerate no nonsense.

"Where have you been, Eddie?" she demanded to know. "And who is that you've got with you?"

"His name's Ezekiel, Ma!" Eddie announced, proudly. "He can play the trumpet. Can we keep him?"

"What's he doing here?"

"He's looking for work."

"Well, you brought him all this way for nothing then, 'cause there's no work to be had on this farm."

"S'cuse me, Ma'am?" said Ezekiel.

"Yes?"

"I'm terrible hungry, Ma'am, and I ain't got nowhere to lay my head. It's looking like it's gonna snow, too. Can't you let me sleep in your barn for tonight? I won't bother nobody, and then I'll move on tomorrow."

"Please, Ma?" begged Eddie.

Mrs. Schneider looked Ezekiel up and down. "Oh, all right," she reluctantly agreed. "You can stay in the barn, but there'll be no trumpet playing. You'll upset my cows, and I have enough trouble getting milk out of them. There are some blankets by the stalls, and I'll send Eddie out with some soup. By the by, just so you know, I keep a loaded shotgun beside my bed."

She hustled her son inside the house, slamming the screen door and door behind her. Ezekiel shook his head, shrugged his shoulders, and walked to the barn. He opened one of its creaky doors, took a sniff and recoiled, then he turned to look resentfully at the warm-looking house.

"Good thing she got that gun," he mumbled to himself, "'cause ain't nothin' else gonna sleep with her in that dress. Look like an old maid. Hee, hee."

The next morning, Ezekiel rose before the rooster and set to work. There were only seven cows to tend: two Jersey; one Holstein; three scrub; and a scrub calf. He led them to their feeding stalls, secured the mature cows with stanchions, and tied the calf to its mother. He watered them and poured salted feed into their troughs. While they ate, he sweet-talked them and hooked them up to the hoses. He turned on the mechanical dairymaid and shook with laughter as the milk flowed into the stainless steel vat. When it slowed to a trickle, he removed the hoses and fed the cows some hay. He put them out to exercise and returned to the barn to clean out the manure from the gutters. He swabbed down the creosoted-wood floors, and he laid up pans of milk to set for cream on the dairy shed shelves. When sleepy-eyed Eddie stumbled into the barn, he found his morning's work completed.

"Wow!" he exclaimed. "Wait'll Ma sees this!"

Mrs. Schneider was impressed, although she tried hard not to show it. She fought a smile as she walked the length of the barn and inspected each stall. Finally, she turned to Ezekiel and asked him where he had learned about dairying.

"There's a big farm outside of Saint Louis, Ma'am," he answered. "I used to spend my summers working there."

"I see." Mrs. Schneider tilted her head to the side, and for a moment, she looked vulnerable. "I can't offer you more than room and board, Ezekiel, but you're welcome to stay, if you want. You can't sleep in the house, of course, on account of what folks would say, but we can fix up a space in the loft. When my husband was alive, we had some men sleep up there, and they said it was dry enough."

"That'll be fine," he told her. "I'll stay on for awhile."

"That's settled then," she said, folding her arms. "Better wash up and come in the house. Breakfast is almost ready."

With a strapping man on the farm, life got easier for Mrs. Schneider and her son. Ezekiel got up before the sun rose, and he worked until long after it set. He seemed to enjoy his work and was always polite and cheerful. He was a praying man, too. More than once, Mrs. Schneider caught him on his knees in the barn, and she was touched to hear her name in his prayers.

In time, she allowed him to play his trumpet—and how that man could play! She'd never heard such sweet tones come out of a brass instrument. He lulled her into contentment with his mellow, plaintive improvisations, and he also got her stirred up and nervous playing his frenetic bebop. He sometimes got too carried away with seductive calls on his horn. When he did, she would frown, give him the evil eye, and bid him an abrupt good night.

She thought his remarkable talent should be shared, so she let him take the truck into Waukesha on Saturday nights to play in a club called The Heppin' Horn. He offered to take her along, but she declined. She wasn't a drinking woman, she told him, and she didn't care to be around it. She didn't want her son around it, either, but that didn't stop Eddie. He climbed into the back of the truck one night in early July and covered himself with a tarp. Ezekiel didn't discover him until they pulled up outside The Heppin' Horn.

"Whatchu doin'?" cried Ezekiel. "You tryin' to get me lynched? Your ma is gonna be fit to be tied."

"Aw, she won't even know I'm gone, eh?" Eddie jumped out of the truck. "She sleeps like a slab of granite."

"You better hope she does, boy, for both our sakes."

Ezekiel never heard such catcalling as when they stepped into the club, but perhaps it was to be expected. All the patrons were black. The men wore double-breasted suits, and the women were dressed in taffeta and fox fur. Poor Eddie stood there, white as a ghost, in his bib overalls and muddy boots. One of the men yelled something that Eddie couldn't understand, and the folks hollered and squealed.

"Why you draggin' that skinny farm boy in here?" Cato, the bartender, asked Ezekiel. "He ain't old enough to drink."

"Then get him a Co-Cola," snapped Ezekiel. He was annoyed and embarrassed. "And leave the boy alone. He ain't near as white as he looks."

Eddie took a stool in a dark corner, and everybody soon dismissed him from their minds. He was free to relax and watch all the fun. There was much drinking, hooting, and carrying on, and there was a lot of dancing too, once Ezekiel started blowing his horn. The women cussed and sassed their men, who pulled them to their laps and kissed them to shut them up. The party was in full swing when a large woman threw open the front door and entered. In a voice that dwarfed the din of the crowd, she called for complete silence. The revelry came to a standstill, and the horn went flat and ceased.

"Where is he?" she shouted, pushing shoulders out of her way. "I know he's here! I saw his name on one of them flyers! I done heard his horn! Where is he? Lemme at 'em!"

Ezekiel cowered in a corner, listening to Big Lizzie's voice get closer and closer. One of the taller patrons dared to impede her path and suffered a fist in the eye. He tipped to the ground like a felled tree, and a full-on fight ensued. Feet got to kicking; noses got to bleeding; bottles went flying; and Big Lizzie's carpetbag went swinging. In the middle of this ruckus, Ezekiel took his trumpet and snuck out the back door. He doubled around to the front and grabbed Eddie, and they hopped in the truck.

"Is she behind us?" asked Ezekiel, as they sped down the road.

"I don't think so," Eddie replied, looking out the back window. "I can't see no headlights. Who was that woman anyway?"

"A demon from hell, that's who she is," Ezekiel shook his head in disbelief. "Now how'd that woman find me all the way up here? I guess that means I gotta move on."

"You mean, leave the farm?"

"Ain't got no choice," said Ezekiel. "You saw her. You got a good look at that thing. That woman could tear me in half." He looked at the boy and softened. "Sure will miss you, though. You think your ma will get on all right without me?"

"She managed before, eh?" Eddie curtly reminded him. "Besides, I think she's gonna marry Bob Svenson."

"That inspector from the state board of health?"

"Yep."

"But he's twice her age!"

"Whadda you care?" Eddie turned to face him. "You keep on runnin' and let Mister Svenson take care of Ma. He's got loads of money socked away."

They drove on in miffed silence, as the bumpy, country road passed by in the headlights. About three miles from the Schneider farm, one of their tires blew. The truck swerved, and Ezekiel panicked and over-compensated with the wheel. They dipped off into a field and struck a small cherry tree. When Ezekiel got out to inspect the damage, it was clear to him that the truck wasn't going anywhere that night. He kicked it and cursed it, and then he got tickled at himself and began to giggle.

"You okay?" asked Eddie. "I ain't gonna have to send for a head doctor, am I?"

"You know what we need?" Ezekiel reached in the truck for his case. "We need us some music. There are moments in life, son, when the only thing that can help is a strong dose of the blues. This is one of those moments."

He took out a rag from his back pocket and shined the bell of his horn. He oiled the valves and emptied the spittle, and he licked and stretched his lips until they were moist and limber. He placed the instrument to his mouth and began to blow.

His piece started off as a dirge—a hymn for the broken-hearted. It climbed to a bitter crescendo, then swooped to wallow in filth. It picked itself up again and swaggered for several bars. Then Ezekiel added a mute, and the tune "wah-wahed" in a ribald, saucy strut.

"Quiet!" Eddie suddenly whispered, tugging on Ezekiel's shirttail. "Hold it a minute!"

"Boy, what's wrong with you?" asked Ezekiel irritably. "Don't you know better than to interrupt when music is talkin'?"

"What's that over there?" Eddie pointed to the eastern half of the night sky. "It looks like some kind of a wheel!"

Ezekiel saw the wheel way up in the middle of the air. Its bottom rim spun faster than a top, and colorful lights shone from underneath. It zigged and zagged, and it hovered in spurts as it advanced in their direction. It came to rest above their heads and pulsed with a humming drone.

"It's one of th-th-them flying saucers!" cried Ezekiel, clutching his trumpet to his chest.

"They must've been attracted by your music, eh?" Eddie smiled, and his buckteeth glowed in the dark. "Play 'em another tune."

"Are you crazy? I ain't gonna play nothin'!"

"Why not, if they like it? Are you gonna be a coward all your life?"

"Coward?" Ezekiel spun the boy around to look him in the eyes. "Is that what you think of me?" Eddie didn't answer, which told Ezekiel all he needed to know. He let go of the boy's shoulders and said, "All right, then. I'll play, but I ain't playin' for them. I'm playin' for you."

He put the horn to his lips again and blew a sustained wail. Before he could move on to the next note, a strong beam of light shot down onto the two humans. Eddie was expelled from the pool of radiance by some unseen energy force. He watched from the pasture across the road as Ezekiel was elevated and taken aboard the space craft.

"Help me!" shouted Ezekiel, and then he passed out cold.

When he came to, he was lying strapped to a gurney. A curious lamp was hanging inches from his nose. It floated, alone, with no anchor or cord, and it was intensely bright. He turned his head, squinted his eyes, and strained to make sense of his surroundings.

The walls were round and white with tiny, oval windows, and the floor was covered with hospital-green tiles. Weird girders stamped with hieroglyphs vaulted the domed ceiling. Control panels beeped, flashed, and churned out printed data, and shiny black chairs, void of cushions, sat in a half circle. It all seemed as sterile as the stench of disinfectant that permeated the room.

An eerie feeling came over Ezekiel, as though he were being watched. He looked up towards the lamp and was shocked to see three space aliens leaning over him. They were gray and little, and their skin had the sheen of Mylar. Their eyes were big and black, they had pinholes for noses, and their mouths were the size of quarters. Their heads were disproportionally large, and their digits were elongated and rubbery. They were hideous entities, made all the more frightening because they each carried a hypodermic needle big enough to vaccinate an elephant.

"Greetings, Earthling!" they said together, in helium-high voices.

"Oooooowaaaaaaaah!" screamed Ezekiel.

"Stop that," they told him. "Don't make us get the ray gun."

"The ray gun?" Ezekiel gulped. "What do you critters want with me?"

"That series of vibrations you were producing down on your planet—what is that process called?"

"You mean, the blues?"

"Bluezzz," they repeated. "Do all like specimens produce like vibrations?"

"Uh, no," he answered. "Everybody got their own gift. But I believe anybody can appreciate the blues, if they let themselves."

"We want to produce this 'bluezzz.'"

"That's fine," he said, chuckling. "Let me off this contraption, and I'll be happy to show you some of the basics."

"We do not have the time for manual instruction," they sang out. "We must extract the necessary data from the synapses deep within your brain. Hold still."

"WHAT!" bellowed Ezekiel. "You ain't extractin' nothin' from my body!"

But the aliens ignored his pleas. They jabbed their three needles far up into his nose and began withdrawing a liver-colored soup. Ezekiel lost consciousness.

When he woke moments later, he was astonished to find the aliens playing the blues. One had fashioned a vibraphone from some hospital-green tiles and was using his long index fingers as mallets; another scatted, slow and bruisy; and the third was blowing hot on the trumpet. Their eyes were closed in rapture, and their repulsive little bodies writhed.

But Ezekiel didn't like the thought of alien spit dripping down his beloved trumpet. He galvanized all of his strength and courage and broke free of his restraints. He took back his horn and with one sweep of his arm sent the aliens flying into the control panels. The spacecraft titled and whirled, and alarm bells began to sound. Emergency lights flashed, and water sprinklers were activated. Then, CRASH!

Holding his head, but still carrying his trumpet, Ezekiel emerged from the wreckage. He stepped over the three lifeless gray bodies and stumbled out onto a field. A farmer drove up in a pick-up truck. He got out, looking near as dazed as Ezekiel.

"Where am I?" Ezekiel asked him,

"Why, son, don't you know?" The farmer suddenly beamed with pride. "You're in sunny Roswell, New Mexico!"

Ezekiel was rushed to a White Sands laboratory, where a team of scientists poked and prodded his body. The chief examiner—a Russian doctor who introduced herself as Doctor Sadisky—was the roughest of them all. She clamped onto Ezekiel's chin and jerked his head from side to side; she banged his kneecaps with a rubber hammer; and she shoved her hands underneath him and flipped him like a pancake. She might have continued to torture him all night, had she not been interrupted by a man in military uniform.

"Mister Jones," said the man, as he crossed the room to shake Ezekiel's hand, "I'm Captain Phil Dickens. I'm sorry for your trouble, sir. I understand you've had quite a night."

"May I go home?" Ezekiel asked him.

"Where exactly is your home sir?"

Ezekiel opened his mouth to answer, but no words came out. He was no longer sure what place to call home. He couldn't go back to Saint Louis, and Big Lizzie had probably already tracked him down to the Schneider farm. What he needed was someplace far away to hide and be happy.

"My home is in Japan," he said. "Can you take me there?"

"I don't see why not," replied Captain Dickens. He turned to

184

Doctor Sadisky and leaned close to her ear. "He's lying, of course," he whispered, "but who cares? It suits our needs. We'll stash him in some remote corner of Japan, where the press will never find him. Finish your examination, Doctor, and then give him the serum. You think he'll be open to suggestion?"

"He won't remember a thing about tonight," Doctor Sadisky promised.

"Good. And Doctor?"

"Yes, Captain?"

"What are you doing later?"

And so it happened that Ezekiel began a new life in Japan. He settled on a small island off the coast of Hokkaido, and he opened a joint called The Konnyaku Club. There, he blew his horn nightly. He was a sensation with the local girls. . . until Big Lizzie waded up on the shore.

Chapter 15

GLORIA AND ELVIS

EBEKAH WACKERMAN—A.K.A. GLORIA GORDON—WAS A product of the Hollywood studio system, and some would say its victim. She was "discovered" at a corner drugstore by an octopus disguised as a talent scout. Because she danced and sort of sang, and since she had great gams, the producers routed her into movie musicals. She carved out a career playing gold-digging secretaries, home-wrecking heiresses, and gum-chewing molls. The critics never accorded her the respect they gave to, say, Alice Faye, but the tabloid press took to her because her love affairs made great copy.

When war broke out, she toured with the USO, and the Yanks in Europe couldn't get enough of her. They taped her pinup to their Sherman tanks, and they christened their Mustangs after her. She dated several officers, including a general named "Red" and a lieutenant named "Pip." She finally married Adam Zeltzer, an enlisted man from Brooklyn, but he was killed by friendly fire shortly thereafter.

The war ended, and Gloria went to London to play a gold-digging secretary in Sir Alfred Cockburn's technicolor extravaganza "A Tune To Forget." On the set, she was introduced to the great tragedian Terrence Rennier. He was dashing, silver tongued, and single. Their wedding took place at Stonehenge, and the press ate it up with a spoon. But she found out on her honeymoon that Terrence preferred the company of randy sailors, so she left him for the acclaimed Hollywood director Sam Feldstein.

When Sam was fatally charred on the set of "The Burning of Richmond," Gloria suffered a nervous breakdown and was confined to a sanitarium. She endured a long series of shock treatments, and was frequently thrown into ice baths. Every conceivable psychological drug was forced down her throat, and at one point a lobotomy was discussed. In the end however, she outlived all her doctors. Since no one could remember who she was or why she was there, they let her walk out the door and onto the street.

She was free, but she was broken. Her looks, money, and career had long ago gone down the drain. She had no hope left in her. She didn't bother dolling up, because she no longer believed there was a man alive who would have her. She didn't believe in anything—not heaven, hell, or the weatherman.

Still, she was alive, and she had to eat. She didn't want to end up in another institution, so she took a job as a night receptionist in a sleazy motel. She hated it, but it paid enough to meet her rent and buy her cigarettes, gin, and cat food. That is how her story might have ended, were it not for that now famous incident that occurred on New Year's Eve, 1999.

Of course, the whole world was jumpy and weird that night, and Tinseltown was certainly no exception. There were limos, black ties, and fireworks in Beverly Hills, and there were charity balls in Westwood. The hippies were chanting in Benedict Canyon, and the boys on Santa Monica Boulevard were having one of their parades. But in the no-man's land between East and West Hollywood, the destroyed and twisted combed the streets for crack, cash, and company.

Gloria arrived for work a few minutes late. The buses were running off-schedule, but it was no good trying to explain that to Papa Bob, the bearded, leather-clad biker she relieved. He mumbled profanities under his breath, punched out, and roared off on his Harley to join his buddies and babes at a keg party.

It was around eleven when Conchita came in with a "john." As usual, Conchita's eyes rolled about in their sockets, desperately searching for a point of orientation. Her mouth was lax, and a dollop of spittle foamed in the corner of her glossed lips.

The man was in his twenties and moderately attractive. Gloria had seen a thousand like him. He had probably just come out West from Oklahoma or some such place with dreams of becoming a star. He slurred his words, and his breath reeked of tequila. At Conchita's prompting, he signed in as "Ricky Martin."

"Don't leave a mess," Gloria warned them, as she tossed them a key to the room beside the icemaker. "Happy New Year."

When Conchita and "Ricky" left the office, Gloria opened a big bag of generic corn chips and settled into a Lazy-Boy. She was riveted to the pages of a Jackie Collins novel when the doorbell rang, signaling a new arrival. By rocking her body and pushing off from the arms, she ejected herself from the chair. Her old bones crackled and popped as she moved behind the desk to face the guest. It was Elvis Presley.

He looked just like she'd last seen him on the E! True Hollywood Story. His suit was white and rhinestone-encrusted, and so was his trade-mark cape. He wore sunglasses and lots of gold chains, and his sideburns were marvels to behold. He stood with his hands on his turquoise belt buckle, and one side of his upper lip strove in vain to touch his nostril. He was everything that Elvis should be, and yet Gloria was understand-ably skeptical.

"Just get in from Vegas?" she asked, testing the waters. "I would have thought you impersonators could rack up some bucks on a night like tonight."

"I don't play Vegas anymore," he told her, "and I'm no imper-sonator."

"Right, right." She paused to pick a piece of corn chip from her dentures with her tongue. "Will it be single or double occupancy, Mr.

Presley?"

"Call me Elvis."

"Sure," agreed Gloria. "Single or double, Elvis?"

"I don't want a room, Gloria."

"Listen, don't be yanking my chain," she said, wagging a finger at him. "If you don't want a room, get your ass back out on the... What did you call me? How do you know my name? I don't know what kind of game you're playing Mister, but you oughta know I'm packing a piece."

"Don't be afraid." Elvis pushed his glasses to the tip of his nose and peered out over them. "It's really me. Here, I'll prove it." He sang a few bars of "Love Me Tender."

"What does that prove?" she asked him, when he was done. "That Andy Kaufmann did it better."

"Did not."

"Did too."

"All right then, if I'm not the real Elvis, how come I know so much about you, huh? How come I know about your marriages, your breakdown, and your fifteen minutes of fame?"

"It was more than fifteen, buster!"

"Fine. Twenty."

"Anybody could know that stuff about me," Gloria protested. "You coulda read some magazine."

"Yeah?" Elvis chuckled. "Maybe you haven't noticed, baby, but you're not exactly fodder for the tabloids these days. The public has forgotten you, but I haven't. I'm here to give you a second chance, Gloria."

"Do you mean that you're. . . you're really and truly. . ."

"A hunk, a hunk of burning love?"

"You're Elvis!"

"Thank you very much."

"But you're dead, aren't ya?" Gloria asked, clutching her heart. "Aren't ya?"

"Dead, but not gone," he answered, with a smile. "Elvis will live forever. Don't you believe that?"

"Oh, I believe, Elvis!" cried Gloria, stomping her feet and lifting her palms to Heaven. "I believe!"

"I'm glad to hear that Gloria. I was beginning to think you didn't believe in anything. Why don't you come with me?"

He took her outside to a parked Cadillac convertible, and showed her the registration in her name. There was a cashmere coat in the driver's seat, and it happened to be her size. In the trunk were cartons of cigarettes and cases of gin and cat food, and a bulletproof attaché case containing gold bars and a pouch of cut diamonds.

"I don't know how to thank you," she said, weeping, as Elvis led her back into the office to sit down and catch her breath. "I can't believe all that stuff is mine."

"You'd better believe it," Elvis sternly warned her, "because believing is the one condition on this windfall. If you stop believing, the gig is up, and you'll find yourself in worse condition than before. So, do you believe?"

"I do!" shouted Gloria. "I do!"

"Thank you very much."

He kissed her on the forehead and gave her a thumbs-up. He dropped to the floor in a dramatic pseudo-split, then recovered his cocksure stance. He walked out of the motel office and out of her life forever, but as he did, a voice out of nowhere boomed, "Elvis has left the building!"

When the reporters got hold of the story—and Gloria made sure they did—she was thrust back into the limelight. Headlines like, "Washed-up Star Meets Elvis" and "The King Lives!" were splashed across tabloids and respectable papers alike. She did guest spots on Jay Leno and David Letterman, and she was even a guest VJ for MTV Jams.

Her facelift made the cover of PEOPLE and TALK magazines, and TCM hosted a Gloria Gordon movie marathon during a ratings sweep.

In time, the public proved fickle, and mud began to sling. Her account of that New Year's Eve was hotly debated, especially by those who'd been close to "The King." Her history of mental illness cast serious doubts on her credibility, and she became the favorite punch line of stand-up comedians. The worst moment came when a league of churches picketed the book signing for the release of her autobiography.

But fame, good or bad, was better than invisibility, so Gloria made the most of it. She starred on Hollywood Squares and sold Elvis memorabilia on The Home Shopping Network. An offbeat cult sprang up around her, and in her last days, she became a lightning rod for Elvis sighters, movie musical fans, and sci-fi buffs. She hired a young fitness guru, and the two of them fell in love and set up house in Palm Springs. And when she finally quit this world—peacefully in her sleep—she was the lead story on CNN Headline News.

ABOUT THE AUTHOR

Christopher Leonard, born in 1962, earned a BFA from University of North Carolina at Greensboro. He served as assistant editor of Poor William's Omnibus, a literary monthly in Charleston, South Carolina. He also scripted several theatrical productions including "The Soul of Sugar Dove," and the annual "CHOC Follies" in Orange County, California. Christopher is the pianist-in-residence for the Richmond Hill Inn in Asheville, North Carolina. He lives quietly with his two cats, Ashley and Peyton.

For additional copies, contact:

Richmond Hill Inn
87 Richmond Hill Drive
Asheville, NC 28806
828-252-7313
www.richmondhillinn.com